‖‖‖‖‖‖‖‖‖‖‖‖‖‖‖‖‖‖‖‖‖
◁ **W9-AZG-777**

FROM THE
NANCY DREW FILES

THE CASE: *Find the midnight prowler who's causing a string of nasty "accidents" at Webb Cove Ski Lodge—even if it means ruining a romantic vacation with Ned.*

CONTACT: Liz Whitcomb, *owner of the lodge. She wants Nancy's help—but has she got something to hide?*

SUSPECTS: Luke Ericsen, *the lodge's ski instructor. He's a man with a mysterious—and maybe murderous—past.*

Michael Price, *a handsome, helpful stranger. He saved Nancy from a serious accident. Is he being a white knight? Or does he have a darker motive?*

Gunther, *a cheerful German student enjoying an American vacation. He came to the lodge for fun—or could he be there for revenge?*

COMPLICATIONS: *George Fayne has fallen for Luke Ericsen—with all the blindness of first love. How can Nancy tell her Luke could be a killer? Then a blizzard cuts the lodge off from the rest of the world, and the prowler strikes again. Ned, George, and Nancy find their lives on the line!*

Books in THE NANCY DREW FILES® Series

Available from ARCHWAY Paperbacks

Most Archway Paperbacks are available at special quantity discounts for bulk purchases for sales promotions, premiums or fund raising. Special books or book excerpts can also be created to fit specific needs.

For details write the office of the Vice President of Special Markets, Pocket Books, 1230 Avenue of the Americas, New York, New York 10020.

THE NANCY DREW FILES™

CASE · 3

MURDER ON ICE

Carolyn Keene

AN ARCHWAY PAPERBACK
Published by POCKET BOOKS
New York   London   Toronto   Sydney   Tokyo

This book is a work of fiction. Names, characters, places and incidents
are either the product of the author's imagination or are used fictitiously.
Any resemblance to actual events or locales or persons, living or dead, is
entirely coincidental.

AN ARCHWAY PAPERBACK *Original*

An Archway Paperback published by
POCKET BOOKS, a division of Simon & Schuster Inc.
1230 Avenue of the Americas, New York, N.Y. 10020

Copyright © 1986 by Simon & Schuster Inc.
Cover artwork copyright © 1986 Joseph Cellini
Produced by Mega-Books of New York, Inc.

All rights reserved, including the right to reproduce
this book or portions thereof in any form whatsoever.
For information address Pocket Books, 1230 Avenue
of the Americas, New York, N.Y. 10020

ISBN: 0-671-64194-8

First Archway Paperback printing September 1986

10 9 8 7 6 5 4

NANCY DREW, AN ARCHWAY PAPERBACK and colophon
are registered trademarks of Simon & Schuster Inc.

THE NANCY DREW FILES is a trademark
of Simon & Schuster Inc.

Printed in the U.S.A.

IL 7+

MURDER ON ICE

Chapter

One

A LIGHT SNOW was falling from the overcast February sky as Nancy Drew steered her Mustang expertly along the twisting Vermont road. More snow meant even better skiing! Nancy's blue eyes sparkled at the thought.

Nancy, George Fayne, and Bess Marvin, her two best friends, were looking forward to a really fabulous ski trip. And having Ned Nickerson along would make the vacation just perfect.

"Sorry you decided to come along?" Nancy asked Ned. "The only guy with three girls?"

"You've got to be kidding!" George spoke up before Ned could answer. "Ned knows I'll be hitting the slopes every minute I can, and Bess will have guys falling all over themselves to impress her. And there isn't a mystery in sight!

You and Ned will have plenty of time for snuggling by the fire."

"Really?" Nancy answered innocently. "I thought we were here for skiing."

"How would you like some snow down your neck?" Ned teased.

"Hey," interrupted Bess, "aren't we looking for Webb Cove Road? You just passed it!"

Nancy slowed the blue Mustang and made a careful three-point turn, her reddish blond hair bouncing as she turned her head to check the side-view mirror. She pulled onto the narrow road Bess indicated and proceeded smoothly through the snow. Soon a rustic sign appeared on the left: Webb Cove Road. "Okay, everybody, watch for the sign to the lodge," Nancy said.

Bess's blue eyes met Nancy's in the rearview mirror, and she shook her blond head. "I've heard about snow blindness, but it looks like Nancy's got a bad case of Ned blindness. Pay attention, Nan, and you won't miss any more turns."

"Hah! Look who's talking about boy blindness!" dark-haired George retorted. She and Bess were cousins, but they couldn't have been more different. George, a top athlete, was shy with boys. Bess's favorite sports were shopping and men, not necessarily in that order.

"Okay," Ned exclaimed as Nancy steered around a curve and heavy stone gateposts loomed before them. "This is the place. Webb Cove Lodge!"

Nancy swung through the open gates and

pulled up before a heavy, dark red door. The lodge was long and low, snuggled into a fold of the hill. Its peaked roof looked vaguely alpine, and the overcast skies made the weathered boards seem very dark—like something out of a ghost story, Nancy thought. Then she smiled to herself, realizing that she was automatically seeing things as mysterious!

She parked the car in a small lot and she and her friends piled out.

"All right! The sun's out!" George cried happily. She and Nancy took their skis off the roof carrier and pulled boots out of the backseat. Bess and Ned would have to rent ski equipment. "Let's get checked in and hit the slopes fast!" George said enthusiastically.

As Nancy and the others stepped into the lodge's cozy office, lugging bags and skis, a sturdy, cheerful young woman in jeans and a plaid wool shirt looked up from behind the registration desk. "Welcome to Webb Cove," she said. "You must be the group from River Heights. Come on in. Which one of you is Nancy Drew? Since you made the reservations, you might as well sign in for everybody."

Bess read over Nancy's shoulder as she filled in the registration form. "Name, address, phone and credit card numbers, license plate number . . . hey, you forgot to fill in the blank for occupation. Put down, 'Nancy Drew, Notorious Girl Detective'!"

"Knock it off," Nancy muttered. She hated it when Bess said things like that in front of people she didn't know. Nancy was always modest, even though her detective work had earned her an international reputation.

Nancy left the occupation line blank. "Here you are," she said, handing the registration form back to the woman behind the desk. "Nancy Drew, George Fayne, Bess Marvin, and Ned Nickerson, all present and accounted for."

"Thanks. I'm Liz Whitcomb. I run this place. Best way I know to make a living and still be a ski bum." Liz grinned. "Leave your skis and boots in the entryway. I'll show you to your bunks.

"I'm afraid we don't have porters or the rest of the fancy trimmings you'd have if you stayed up the road at the Overlook—the big resort hotel. But then, most people don't bring many clothes along," she added dryly, watching Bess struggle with her two suitcases. "By the way, if any of you need to rent skis from us, you'd better do it quickly. We have a lot of guests this week so we're short on rentals."

Liz led Nancy and her friends through a large, wood-paneled sitting room. Comfortable sofas covered in red wool plaid were gathered around a big stone fireplace. Sheepskin rugs dotted the slate floors, and sports magazines were piled haphazardly on the tables. At one end of the room, swinging doors led to what sounded like the kitchen. Liz led them through a rustic door at the opposite end of the room that opened onto a corridor.

"As you probably know, this place is dormitory-style," she explained. "Most of our guests are college students and hostelers from overseas. The guys' room is on the left, gals' on the right.

"The ski area, Big Birch, is on the other side of the mountain. An old chair lift will take you to the top. You can connect into the main trails easily there. The schedules for meals and ski classes with our resident instructor are posted in the dorms."

Ned nodded. "The lodge has its own ski instructor?" he asked.

"Not always. Instructors come and go. But we have a good one right now—Luke Ericsen. He showed up a few weeks ago, looking for work. He's a ski bum like me," Liz said, laughing, "and a fantastic athlete and teacher."

She opened the door to the women's bunk room. "Here you are, girls. You'll be able to tell which bunks aren't taken. Let me know if there's anything you need."

Ned caught the sleeve of Nancy's down jacket. "See you on the slopes in a little while, okay? I have to see about renting skis." He waved to the others and followed Liz toward the men's bunk room.

The girls' room was simple but attractive, even if it wasn't, as George remarked, fancy enough to suit Bess's taste. The bunks were built of dark-stained wood and covered with comforters in bright patchwork patterns.

Nancy dropped her suitcase onto the bunk by the back window and sat down beside it, yawning. "Whew! Driving in that snow really tired me out."

"*I* could go for a nap by the fire in the lounge. If only I had somebody cute to curl up with," Bess added wistfully.

Her friends grinned. "Bess, a couple of days from now you'll have boys falling at your feet, just as George said," Nancy reassured her.

"Who wants to wait?" Bess said with a sigh. "It's easy for you to talk, Nancy. Your tall-dark-and-handsome's here with you."

"Face it, Bess, you have a one-track mind," George told her bluntly. "Nancy'd have a good time even if Ned weren't here. *Nancy,*" she added significantly, "likes skiing. A little exercise wouldn't hurt you any."

"Don't remind me," Bess groaned. "I went on a pizza binge last week. I'll probably look like a blimp in my new stretch pants!"

Nancy and George exchanged amused glances. "Maybe you should hunt up that ski instructor," Nancy suggested. "What was his name? Luke something?"

"Ericsen," Bess said promptly.

"Did you take notes, Bess?" George asked, giggling.

Bess grinned. "No, but a handsome ski instructor isn't such a bad idea." She began brushing her long blond hair. "Although he'd probably be more interested in a skiing ace like George."

"For all we know, the guy's middle-aged and has a wife and sixteen kids," George returned, blushing.

Bess gestured for quiet, and they heard a deep voice in the next room.

"Hear that?" Bess's eyes sparkled. "Boys. Hmmm . . . I think I'll wear my new blue ski sweater."

"Happy hunting!" Nancy exclaimed. "I'm going skiing!" She zipped up her jacket, grabbed her mittens, and tramped out the door.

Liz was sitting behind the registration desk as Nancy passed the open door to the office. She rose so quickly that Nancy realized Liz had been waiting for her. "May I speak to you a minute?" she asked quietly. "In private."

"Of course," Nancy said. She stepped into Liz's office. To her surprise, Liz closed the door, then locked it. She turned to Nancy, her face serious.

"Is it true, what your friend said? You're a detective?"

Nancy nodded. "Yes. Why?"

Liz didn't answer at once. A draft of cold air sliced through the cracks around the windows. Something—a tree branch, probably—scratched against the windowpane. It was a faint sound, but Liz jumped as if it were a thunderclap. She whirled around, her face drained of color.

"Liz," Nancy cried, "what is it? There's nothing there."

"I know," Liz answered shakily. "I guess it was just a tree branch."

"But that's not what frightened you, is it? Please tell me," Nancy urged gently.

Liz swallowed and forced a smile. "Look at

THE NANCY DREW FILES

me, jumping out of my skin like that! A week ago, I'd have said I was never afraid of anything."

"But now you are afraid. Has something happened?"

Liz looked nervously at Nancy. "It started last week," she began. "I came down here to get something in the middle of the night, and I saw a face staring through that window. It was a monster's face—no body, no nose or mouth—a face that could scare you to death!"

Chapter

Two

"WHAT?" NANCY EXCLAIMED. "How could that be?"

"Well," Liz said, "that's just the way it looked at first. The guy had his face pressed against the glass, so his features were all distorted. And he was probably wearing dark clothes, which was why he seemed to have no body."

"He?" Nancy asked. "How do you know it was a man?"

Liz flushed. "Oh, his . . . his size," she said uncomfortably. "It's a high window."

Nancy frowned. Liz seemed terribly flustered. "Did you notice anything else about him?" she asked.

"Yes. I could see that he had blue eyes and blond hair."

"You're sure? You could tell that in the dark?"

"Oh." Liz cleared her throat. "Yes, well . . . pretty sure."

"All right. That should help me," said Nancy.

"But, Nancy," Liz went on, sounding frightened, "he was trying to get inside!"

Nancy felt a shiver run up her spine, but she made her voice matter-of-fact. "What did you do?"

"I went straight to the back door," Liz answered grimly. "By the time I unlocked it and opened it, there was no one outside! But there were ski tracks in the snow beneath the window, and nobody has any reason to be messing around that part of the yard on skis!"

"Could it have been somebody from another lodge just checking the place out?" Nancy suggested.

"In the middle of the night?" Liz sighed dramatically. "Nancy, I'm frightened. I don't like the idea of somebody poking around here. Aside from the Overlook, which is about two miles away, at the bottom of the Big Birch chair lift, we're very isolated here."

"It's creepy, for sure," Nancy said in a calm tone of voice, "but it doesn't sound too dangerous. I mean, that guy didn't actually do anything and he hasn't come back . . . has he?"

"That's just it. He has!" Liz shot an apprehensive look toward the door. "Last night—late—I saw a figure skiing away from the lodge. And this morning, it looked to me like the lock to the kitchen door had been tampered with.

"There's something else, too. I've received two

10

phone calls in the last three days asking for somebody named John. The first time, I said we had nobody here by that name, and the caller became very angry, almost violent-sounding. The next time, he hung up on me."

"Let's go back to those ski tracks you found. Where did they come from?" Nancy asked. "Did you follow them?"

"Yes," replied Liz. "They came from the little trail that connects us with the Big Birch ski area and the Overlook Hotel. Those tracks had to have been made after the snowstorm stopped—and that was after two A.M." Liz looked at Nancy. "You're a detective, you tell me. What was somebody doing prowling around here at that time of night? I can't think of any pleasant reason."

Nancy nodded soberly. If someone wanted to get inside Webb Cove Lodge, it would probably be fairly easy . . . and that meant danger!

"I don't scare easily," Liz said, "but that face at the window was terrifying."

Nancy knew what was coming. "And you're asking me to do some detecting for you."

"Yes!" Liz replied emphatically. "I want to hire you, but I want you to keep a low profile. I'm not going to the police unless I have to. Rumors about a prowler won't do my lodge any good."

"This prowler doesn't sound like a regular thief," Nancy said slowly. "Liz, why do *you* think he was trying to get in here?"

"I haven't the faintest idea," Liz answered. "If he just wanted to steal, the Overlook Hotel has a lot more guests, and richer ones. It doesn't make sense."

"Well, I'll be glad to do what I can," Nancy said.

"Thank you very much." Liz unlocked the door. "Now, go hit the slopes. After last night's snowstorm, the skiing should be great."

Nancy stepped into the entryway where she and George had left their ski things. She buckled herself into her clunky ski boots, then grabbed her skis and poles and hurried outside into the dazzling sunlight.

As she fumbled for her sun goggles, Nancy caught sight of a male figure in a blue ski suit silhouetted against the sun. I might as well get acquainted, Nancy decided, especially now that I'm supposed to be checking things out. She walked over to the guy and stood her skis in the snow. "Hi," she said. "My name's Nancy."

He turned to face her. He had blond hair and piercing blue eyes. "Hello," he replied. "I'm Luke Ericsen, the ski instructor here."

"Oh," Nancy exclaimed, "I've heard about you. Liz told me you're very good."

"I am."

That brought the conversation to a crashing halt. Luke neither spoke again nor moved. You may be a good skier, Nancy thought, but you're a real snob. She glanced back at the lodge, then toward the trail leading to the ski lift, hoping to catch sight of Ned.

Nancy waited for several minutes, but Ned didn't appear. Finally, she laid her skis on the snow and snapped her boots into them. "I guess I'll head for the chair lift," she declared, half to Luke, half to herself.

"No!" the ski instructor barked. "I have to check it to make sure it's working all right."

"Is something wrong with it?" Nancy asked.

"No, but it's my responsibility to check it each week and make sure it's safe. You'll have to wait until I'm done before you go skiing."

Nancy looked down at her skis and made a face. This guy was definitely a pain. "Isn't there another lift around here? I'm dying to hit the slopes."

"There's a rickety old rope tow I use when I'm checking the chair lift," Luke admitted, gesturing toward a small clearing nearby. "But it's a very steep trail and I'm not letting anybody except an expert mess around on it."

"What makes you think I'm not an expert?" Nancy said hotly, but Luke turned away without answering.

At that moment, Ned stepped out of the lodge. "Hey, Nancy," he called, hurrying up to her. Then he turned to the ski instructor. "I'm Ned Nickerson," he said with a smile. "Are you Luke Ericsen?"

"That's right," Luke replied briefly.

"I was planning to rent some equipment, but Liz told me you have an old pair of skis and boots you're looking to sell. If the boots fit me and I like the way the skis feel, I might be interested in buying them. How about letting me try them out for the day?"

13

Luke just nodded and strode back into the lodge.

Ned whistled. "Obviously a man of few words."

"The fewer the better, if you ask me," Nancy answered. "Why don't you go get the skis? I'll meet you at the top of the mountain in half an hour." She was determined to go skiing right away. She'd just take the old rope tow. She was a good skier. And after all, Luke was planning to take the rope tow himself.

As Ned followed Luke into the lodge, Nancy picked up her poles and headed for the tow.

She found the start button, pushed it, and watched the tow line begin to move smoothly up the mountain. Placing her skis in the faint tracks in the snow, Nancy grabbed the rope and let herself be pulled swiftly up, her skis sliding easily across the packed powder. It had been years since she'd been on a rope tow, and she'd forgotten that it was kind of fun skiing uphill. But it brought back another vague memory—of something not very pleasant. . . .

All at once, Nancy saw a blue-suited skier farther up the slope, waving wildly. Smiling, Nancy lifted one hand off the tow rope and waved back. Bess should be here, she thought. Half an hour after we arrive, the boys are getting friendly!

Then she frowned. It wasn't a friendly wave. The man began skiing swiftly down the gorge. He executed a complicated maneuver, jerked to a

14

stop, and shouted something frantically to Nancy.

But what? He was too far away for her to make out what he was saying.

All at once, Nancy realized what the feel of the rope tow reminded her of. The memory was from years ago, when she was a kid . . . ice skating, playing crack the whip, holding onto a chain of other skaters . . . then suddenly being whipped off that human rope, hard and fast. The wind stung Nancy's face, and the sun goggles impeded her vision. She jerked one hand out of its mitten and pulled the goggles off. Then, squinting with concentration, she scanned every inch of the tow line that she could see and slid her cold fingers along the rope.

Then Nancy caught her breath. Just beyond her reach she could see a spot that was definitely thinner than the rest of the rope. Several strands had parted and now, because of her weight, the rest of them were beginning to fray.

All right, thought Nancy, all I have to do is let go of the rope and stop moving. She loosened her grip.

But at that very moment, the rope broke with a sickening snap. The force whipped her through the air like a rag doll, throwing her toward a massive birch tree.

In a kaleidoscope of confused, blurred images, Nancy saw the frozen slope rise up to meet her.

The rest was darkness.

Chapter

Three

NANCY WAS SOMEPLACE dark, cold, and lonely. The wind whistled, and a shower of ice stung her face as she struggled back to consciousness. She lay half buried in the drifts of snow. *Ned,* she thought achingly.

But Nancy wasn't alone. Gradually she realized that someone was bending over her, urging her to wake up. It was a man's voice, but it wasn't Ned's.

"Come on, *fight!*" Two hands shook her shoulders roughly. Nancy tried to wrench herself away, but the hands still held her. Then the voice spoke again, but it sounded different—concerned and anxious. "Open your eyes. Come on," it said gently.

Nancy's eyelids felt as if they'd frozen together. She was cold, so cold. She drew her breath in. Slowly, she forced her eyes open and looked toward the bright sky.

Between her face and the light was a dark blur that, as her vision cleared, became the face of an unfamiliar young man. It was a handsome face, with blue eyes the same color as his sleek ski suit and topped with a mop of curly blond hair.

"Are you all right?" asked the young man.

"I think so," Nancy murmured. She moved her head tentatively, and it pounded painfully. Then a wave of nausea swept over her, and the blackness threatened to close in again.

Nancy wasn't completely unconscious, though, and she could dimly make out voices through the haze.

"Haven't seen you since the Broken Leg Café," a second male voice was saying. Even in her stupor, Nancy was sure she knew that voice. After a few moments of confusion, she realized it belonged to Luke Ericsen, the ski instructor.

Nancy felt the stranger's grip on her shoulders slacken. Slowly, painfully, she opened her eyes just enough to peek through her lashes. Luke Ericsen was standing over her, looking directly at the stranger with the curly hair.

There was a queer expression on the stranger's face—more alarmed, even, than when he had looked at Nancy a moment ago. Then her vision blurred and once again she sank back into darkness.

The next thing Nancy felt was a cold, tingling

17

sensation on her face. Her eyes opened more easily this time. Luke was kneeling beside her, rubbing snow into her face.

Nancy jerked her head away to avoid the next dose. As she did so, pain exploded in starbursts behind her eyes.

"Don't move like that until you're sure nothing's broken," Luke said sharply.

"I think I'm all right," Nancy said weakly.

"Move your legs slowly, one at a time."

Nancy moved her right one, then her left, and groaned.

"Hurts, doesn't it?" Luke said brusquely. "That's what you get for not listening to me."

Nancy let Luke's comment pass. "Where did your friend go?" she asked.

There was a split second of silence. "What friend?" Luke asked blankly.

Too blankly, Nancy decided. "The guy who saw the rope breaking and warned me," Nancy said deliberately. Then another question occurred to her. The stranger had been farther up the slope, far enough away so that Nancy couldn't understand his words when he shouted to her. How could he *possibly* have seen the rope fraying from that distance?

There was another silence. Then Luke said, "There was nobody else here. You really must have hit your head hard."

Her head was definitely throbbing. Nancy explored it with her fingers and found a bump— and agonizing pain. Could I have imagined that man? she wondered. Then a shout broke into her thoughts.

"Nancy!"

Ned's familiar yell. Nancy sat up painfully to see Ned, George, and Bess running up the mountain toward her.

In another minute, Ned was by her side, his arms around her in a concerned hug. "Are you okay?" he demanded huskily.

"Mmmm," Nancy murmured. "Luckily, I know that the best thing to do when you're falling is just to go limp. I only wish I hadn't hit my head in the process!"

"Good thing you knew what you were doing," George said seriously.

"Knew what she was doing?" Luke cut in. "If your friend here really knew what she was doing, she wouldn't have been on that tow in the first place! I told her not to take it."

"Oh." George frowned slightly at Nancy. Then she turned to Luke and threw him a shy smile.

The young ski instructor glanced quickly at George. "I'm glad *you* understand what I'm talking about. Maybe you can talk some sense into your friend here." He shot Nancy a disgusted look, as he hurriedly put on his skis. Then, abruptly, he turned and headed down the slope.

"Now, why is he going in that direction?" Nancy said thoughtfully, as Ned and George helped her to her feet. "I thought he had to check the chair lift. Maybe he's going after that other guy."

"What other guy?" Bess asked.

Quickly, Nancy told her friends about the man who had warned her. "I don't care what Luke says," she finished up. "There was someone else here, and he was the one who saved me."

"Luke claimed there *wasn't* anyone else?" Ned asked thoughtfully.

"Right." Nancy rubbed her head. Suddenly her hand froze. Her conversation with Liz came rushing back to her. . . . A stranger at the lodge, trying to get inside.

Suddenly alert, Nancy thought, *two* blond, blue-eyed strangers appearing out of nowhere at the lodge—that's just one coincidence too many for me. I'll lay odds that the stranger who scared Liz and the one who saved me are the same guy. But, Nancy realized, now I'm not sure if that stranger is someone to be afraid of.

"Listen, everyone," Nancy suddenly exclaimed. "Something funny is going on here." She told them about Liz's prowler and how the lock had been tampered with. "I don't know what it's all about, but I think it has something to do with the man who saved me and that awful Luke Ericsen. Luke's acted a little oddly, don't you think?"

Just then, Nancy and her friends were interrupted by a shout.

"Hello there!" a young man called out, making his way toward them on cross-country skis. Liz skied up behind him.

"Gunther!" Ned waved. He turned to the others. "I met him in the dorm," he explained.

"He's from Germany, and he's taking a semester off from school to travel through the United States."

Gunther and Liz glided to a stop beside them, and general introductions followed.

"Why don't you rent some cross-country skis and join us?" Gunther asked. He had brown hair and warm brown eyes that were already, Nancy noticed with amusement, fixed on Bess.

Bess, the dedicated nonathlete, beamed back. "Maybe I'll try it . . ." she said.

Nancy saw Liz stifle a smile.

"You can borrow my skis," Liz offered. "Gunther would be a great teacher for you, Bess. He's fantastic on both downhill and cross-country skis. He's part of an alpine rescue team back in Germany."

"Borrow Liz's skis, and I will show you what a pleasure outdoor sports can be," Gunther urged.

"Well . . ." Bess's dimples started to show.

"Why don't we all go back to the lodge first?" Ned interrupted. "Nancy just had a bad fall."

Alarm leaped into Liz's eyes. "Are you all right? What happened?"

"The rope tow broke," Ned said grimly.

"Oh, no!" Liz gasped. She shot Nancy a questioning look. "Do you think this has anything to do with . . ."

Nancy answered with a faint shrug that made her shoulder throb. "I'll explain later," she said quietly, not wanting to discuss the strange incident in front of Gunther.

"Come back to the lodge," Liz said, concerned. "Some hot chocolate would do you good."

Ned helped Nancy down the hill and into the lounge, and then he and Gunther went off to find an ice pack and make some cocoa. While they were gone, George, Bess, and Liz helped Nancy out of her ski boots as she lay down on one of the couches.

"Okay," Liz said, firmly closing the door. "I want to know exactly what went on out there."

"First of all," said Nancy, "you should know that I already told Bess, George, and Ned what you told me in the office. Oh, it's all right," she rushed on, seeing the look of alarm on Liz's face. "They help me with all my cases."

Liz relaxed and Nancy continued, "Anyway, I'm not quite sure what happened on the slope. The rope must just have been worn through."

"How awful!" Liz exclaimed.

"Fortunately, that man somehow saw that the line was frayed and gave me some warning."

"What man?" Liz asked, then caught her breath. "The prowler?"

"I don't know," Nancy replied. "But if so, we could certainly use more prowlers like him. If the rope had snapped before I was prepared, I could have been badly hurt. . . . And he was very concerned after I hit my head."

"I can't say as much for that ski instructor," Bess put in indignantly. "He was so rude! And he didn't even act worried! Who *is* that creep, anyway? If he's such a hotshot skier, why isn't he hitting the big-time competitions?"

A strange, startled look sprang onto George's face.

"Luke's a good skier and a good instructor," Liz said, as if trying to be fair. "He's very careful, too. That's why it's hard for me to understand why he didn't see that frayed rope before we had an accident!"

"I really don't understand you, Bess!" George exclaimed. "When you're in a position of responsibility like Luke is, you have to set down rules."

She turned to Nancy. "No wonder he was mad! How could he know that you're a great skier and that you're used to handling dangerous situations? Besides, he was right, Nancy. You *should* have waited to use the chair lift. If you *had* been badly hurt, he would have been responsible—"

George broke off abruptly. The others were staring at her, openmouthed. George turned scarlet. "I . . . I'll be back later," she muttered. She hurried out, banging the door behind her.

"What's with *her?*" Bess asked in amazement.

"If you ask me," Nancy said, "George has fallen for our bad-natured ski instructor, and fallen hard. Didn't you see the way she was looking at him on the slope?"

Bess looked bewildered. "But George never gets crushes."

"There's always a first time," Liz said with a grin. "Nancy, I'll go get you some aspirins. Be back in a minute." She left the lounge.

Nancy pressed her hands against her temples, trying desperately to make her head stop pounding. She needed to think—about Liz's prowler, the broken tow rope, Luke, and her mysterious rescuer. And now George.

Ned and Gunther came in with the cocoa and an ice pack just as Liz was returning with the aspirin. "About your friend George," Liz said, "I saw her going up the chair lift with Luke just now. . . . I have some work to do—see you later. Let me know if you need anything else." She disappeared into the passageway.

Nancy groaned. "Wouldn't you know that when George finally does fall in love, she does it in a big way. And with Luke Ericsen, of all people!"

"Don't jump to conclusions," Ned said with a laugh. He handed Nancy the ice pack. "George is an athlete. Luke is an athlete. She just understands where he's coming from, that's all."

"You're an athlete. How do you feel about Luke?"

"Hmmm." Ned bit his lip thoughtfully.

"Let's hit the slopes and look for them," Nancy suggested between sips of hot chocolate.

Ned hesitated. "Are you sure you're up to it?"

"I'm okay," Nancy lied. She knew if she told Ned how she really felt, he'd never let her go investigating the mysterious Luke Ericsen.

"Bess and I could meet you later," Gunther suggested. "I want to give her some cross-country skiing lessons."

"Great!" Bess flashed Gunther a dazzling smile.

"Excellent! I will go find the skis Liz promised

you." Gunther took off across the lounge, whistling.

Ned looked at Nancy. "Did my ears deceive me? Bess actually said 'great' to going out in the cold and exercising? You don't suppose she *likes* Gunther?"

"Not so loud!" Bess protested, giggling. Then her face sobered. "I don't know if I should *let* myself like him. He's going back to Germany at the end of the semester."

"Since when has Bess Marvin stayed in love with the same guy for a whole semester anyway?" Nancy asked, amused.

"True," Bess admitted. "But I never plan it that way."

Nancy buckled her boots on once again and went outside to put on her skis while Ned snapped his boots into the skis he'd borrowed from Luke.

"Well," said Nancy, as she and Ned headed slowly for the lift, "obviously Luke has finished checking the chair lift if he and George already took it up the mountain. I hope we run into those two," she added.

Nancy and Ned took the next chair up and sat quietly for a moment, watching the snow-covered trees move past them. The cold air helped to clear Nancy's head, and soon she was enjoying the feeling of whizzing down the slopes. But even though Nancy and Ned skied the entire afternoon, they never ran into George and Luke.

"They're probably hot-dogging down the hardest slope on the mountain," Ned commented.

"It doesn't matter," Nancy said. "We'll catch up with them back at the lodge."

But when Nancy and Ned returned to Webb Cove Lodge, George was nowhere to be found. In fact, she didn't appear until everyone had gathered around the long table in the lounge for dinner. Then she marched in, her color high, and spent the entire meal ignoring Nancy and talking to the other guests at the lodge, most of whom were college students.

She's mad at me, Nancy realized dully, because she knows I'm suspicious of Luke. Nancy chewed her food without really tasting it, feeling slighted and unhappy.

Only later, as she lay sleeplessly in her bed, did Nancy manage to push thoughts of George out of her mind. Unfortunately, those thoughts were replaced with even more troublesome ones. Liz's description of the hideous face pressed against the office window came back to her vividly.

If the prowler really was the same person who had saved her, she was inclined to trust him. After all, he'd warned her about the breaking rope.

And if he really wanted to get into the lodge, he probably could have done so already. Liz's locks, Nancy had noticed, wouldn't be hard to pick. Maybe he had a good reason for looking around Webb Cove . . . and maybe that reason was Luke Ericsen!

They know each other, Nancy thought, that is, if the blond stranger really is Liz's prowler. But Luke hadn't wanted her to realize that. Why?

Nancy lay very still, her head still aching a little from her fall. There were no sounds except the steady breathing of the sleepers in the other bunks. Then Nancy's sharp ears detected a faint crackling sound outside.

A shiver ran down her back as a current of cold air eddied through the cracks in the window frame.

Nancy turned toward the window—and froze. The shade wasn't pulled down all the way . . . and she could see someone at the window. Then, as quickly and silently as it had come, the figure slipped away.

Nancy rose to her knees on the bed. Cautiously, she peeped outside.

No one was there.

There was only wind, moonlight, and snow—and scarring the snow, as if etched by a giant's finger, were letters a yard long. They spelled: MURDERER.

Chapter

Four

THE MESSAGE IN the snow was the first thing Nancy remembered the next morning. She knelt on her bed and looked out the window, but the letters were gone, perhaps swept away by the wind.

What had it meant? Could someone at Webb Cove really be a murderer? Just as important, who had written the letters in the snow, and why?

Nancy didn't have any answers, so she decided not to say anything about what had happened until she could talk to Liz and Ned alone. She showered, dressed, and went to breakfast.

The guests sat around the table in the lounge, eating and talking so excitedly about getting in a good day of skiing that Nancy couldn't help but feel a little better. Glasses clinked, silverware rattled, and the enormous piles of pancakes disappeared rapidly.

"These are great," Ned exclaimed as Liz came in from the kitchen with another platter.

"Good! Have some more!" Liz said cheerfully. She caught Nancy's eye. "How are you feeling after your fall?"

"Fine, except for a few aching muscles. I'd like to speak to you in a little while, though."

"Sure. Right after breakfast." Liz set the pancake platter in front of Bess, who eyed it despairingly.

"If I eat another helping, I'm going to have to ski all day just to work it off," she moaned.

"I'll be glad to give you some more lessons," Gunther said gallantly.

Ned choked on his own second helping and Nancy kicked his ankle warningly. Then she sent a mischievous glance toward George. To her dismay, George turned away and asked loudly, "Is Luke teaching any advanced classes today?"

A prickle ran down Nancy's spine. So George was still giving her the cold shoulder.

"Sure," Liz answered. "He's out fixing that broken rope tow. Why don't you hunt him up?"

"I think I will." George pushed her chair back and got up to leave.

"Why don't you wait for us?" Nancy called.

"You go ahead and finish your breakfast. I'll see you around," George replied abruptly, and walked out.

Suddenly Nancy wasn't interested in her breakfast anymore. But she was definitely interested in the mysterious Luke Ericsen. "Does Luke stay here at the lodge?" she asked casually.

Liz nodded. "He has a room upstairs."

"Oh. Where's he from?"

"He told me he's from some little town up in Maine. And that," Liz said frankly, "is about all anybody knows. But it's been a big help having him around. Less work for me. At least he doesn't hang around the Overlook all the time, the way most of the ski bums do!" She disappeared into the kitchen.

"What's that place like, anyway?" Bess asked. "I hear it's got a great nightclub."

"Perhaps we could—how do you say, 'check it out'?—some evening," Gunther said quickly. He looked at Ned. "Maybe you and Nancy would like to come, too?"

"Definitely," Ned agreed.

Nancy nodded. She wanted to look around the hotel to see if she could get a lead on the tall blond stranger. And maybe learn some more about Luke.

Out loud, she said, "Come on, Ned, help me clear some of the dishes." She stacked the empty plates, and she and Ned took them to Liz in the kitchen.

"What's up?" Liz asked. "Shall we talk in my office?"

"That might be a good idea," Nancy replied. She and Ned followed Liz into her office.

When they were settled with the door shut, Nancy said, "You two better steel yourselves, because this is a real shocker. The prowler came back last night and he left a message in the snow. It said—get this—MURDERER."

"Wow," Ned said softly.

"That's crazy!" Liz exploded—a bit too loudly, Nancy thought. "How could there be a murderer at Webb Cove—at *my* lodge! There haven't been any murders around here—"

"Calm down, Liz," Nancy said. "I wouldn't put much stock in some weird message left in the snow in the middle of the night. But I do intend to find out what's going on here."

"Have you got any ideas yet?" Ned asked.

"Maybe," Nancy replied. "I can't help feeling that the blond guy who warned me about the rope was your prowler. That little ski trail he was on leads only to Webb Cove Lodge, and we know he's not staying here."

"Why do you think he left the message?" Liz wondered.

"Well," Nancy began slowly, "he warned me once—about the tow—so maybe he's trying to warn me, or all of us—about someone he thinks is dangerous."

"And could that someone just possibly be Luke Ericsen?" Ned asked. "You said he deliberately denied knowing our mystery man."

Nancy was silent for a moment. "We don't know much about Luke. I'd certainly hate to accuse him of anything before we have proof. After all, we don't even know if a murder really has been committed! I would say, though, that we should keep an eye on him."

"Both eyes," Ned agreed.

"Maybe I should fire him," Liz said slowly. "Just to get him out of here. . . ."

Nancy frowned. Why would Liz suggest something so drastic? But all she said was, "No, then we'd never solve the mystery. Besides, we don't *know* that he's done anything. And you don't have any cause to fire him."

Ned smiled faintly. "Nancy, you're becoming obsessed with yet another case. Do you think we'll *ever* go on a vacation without having to share it with thieves, kidnappers, or murderers?"

Nancy sighed. Ned was trying to be good-natured, but she got the message. He was tired of playing second fiddle to every mystery that came along. She couldn't blame him for feeling like that. But how could she sit still if there might really be a murderer in the lodge?

"Someday, we'll have a real vacation, I promise," Nancy said. "But for now, we have a ski instructor to follow. And on the slopes, that's not going to be easy."

Ned grinned. "Well, let's hit the mountain."

"Liz, don't worry. We'll get to the bottom of this," Nancy promised as she and Ned left the office and headed for the bunk rooms.

When Nancy reached the women's dorm, she found Bess eyeing several combinations of pants, sweaters, and vests, which she had spread out on her bunk. "Don't tell me you're changing again!" Nancy groaned.

"I think I ate too many pancakes for these pants," Bess said ruefully, looking down at her tight violet corduroys. "And this sweater doesn't really go with any other pants."

"Forget clothes for a minute. I need to talk to you about something serious." Nancy sat down on her bed. Swiftly she outlined everything that had happened, from the message in the snow to her conversation with Liz and Ned. "Keep quiet about it," she finished. "Liz doesn't want rumors getting out."

"You're going to tell George, aren't you?" Bess asked.

"I don't know," Nancy answered, and sighed. "George gets defensive the minute any of us says a word about Luke. Besides, she's already mad at me."

"She's flipped over him," Bess said bluntly.

"And I don't like it." Nancy's eyes darkened. "Bess, keep an eye on her, will you?"

Bess nodded as she chose a new outfit. "You can count on it."

Nancy and Bess met Ned outside. "I have to wait for Gunther," Bess said. "He's going to give me my first downhill ski lesson."

"Okay," Nancy said with a smile. "Have fun! Ned and I are going to take the chair lift up to Big Birch."

"Remember," Ned added wickedly, "that is your left ski. This is your right ski. This is a pole . . ."

"How can you *stand* him?" Bess complained to Nancy.

Nancy laughed. "Oh, I manage—but just barely!"

Bess shook her head and went back inside to look for Gunther.

Ned looked at Nancy in mock anger. "You just barely manage, huh?"

"Well, a little more than barely," Nancy conceded, laughing. "Come on, let's go." She started toward the lift.

The chair-lift ride to Big Birch was so beautiful that Nancy almost felt sad. It would have been so much fun for her and Ned to be at Webb Cove without a mystery hanging over them!

The lift neared the top of the mountain, and traveled smoothly over one of Big Birch's expert slopes.

"Hey, look over there," Ned cried, pointing. "Luke seems to be holding a private little advanced technique class down there. Very exclusive."

Nancy glanced down at the slope. There were George and Luke, obviously as engrossed in each other as they were in skiing. "Terrific," she muttered, squinting. "We'll have to move fast to catch them. Think you can keep up with me, Ned? This is one of the toughest trails," she teased.

"Don't get cute!" Ned retorted. "Remember, I beat you the last time we raced!"

"The *only* time we raced," Nancy answered.

"Then how about a rematch?" Ned said promptly. "Since you're feeling so cocky. I think I can handle the trail."

"If that's a challenge, you're on!"

The chair lift reached the top of the mountain,

and Nancy and Ned got off. The slopes were growing crowded as the morning sun turned the hills a dazzling white.

Ned skied over to the side of the slope and adjusted his boot buckles. "How do you like Luke's ski equipment?" Nancy asked. "It's really top quality."

"It feels good to me. I just might end up buying it from him."

"Isn't it a little unusual for a ski bum to have not one, but two pairs of first-rate professional skis?" Nancy asked.

Ned laughed. "Clickety-click," he said, tapping Nancy's forehead with his index finger. "Your wheels are always turning."

Nancy smiled, batting away Ned's arm. "Well, *don't* you think so?" she persisted. "I mean, Luke's obviously a terrific skier, but I've watched him and his movements are kind of quirky. I think he favors his right leg a little."

Ned nodded. "I noticed that, too. Could be from an old ski accident."

"Ned, think about this picture for a moment and see if it fits Luke. A guy loves skiing, but an injury keeps him from becoming a real pro. He doesn't want to admit it, though, so he keeps himself supplied with the best ski equipment available and acts like a big cheese."

"Makes sense," Ned admitted. "And George is falling for his delusions of grandeur. You'd think she had more sense than that."

"Love sure *is* blind sometimes," Nancy murmured.

"Now what does *that* mean?" Ned demanded teasingly.

"Oh . . . nothing! Hey, slowpoke, better ski fast if you want to catch me!" And with that, Nancy pushed off, heading down the slope in a flurry of glittering snow.

Behind her she heard Ned let out a surprised bellow, and then he was after her. Nancy shot a glance over her shoulder just in time to see him swoop down and pass her with only inches to spare. He shot ahead, zooming through a couple of quick turns before coming to a perfect parallel stop a little farther down the slope.

Nancy waved one of her ski poles as she shot by him. She could feel him racing after her.

Ned put on a burst of speed and shot past Nancy again. She could tell that he was determined to win the race. Nancy watched the taut lines of his body as he skipped from mogul to mogul.

But suddenly, with a cry of pain, Ned flipped face forward into the snow. He tumbled down the hill, one ski coming off and then the other flying after him.

Horror-struck, Nancy streaked down to where Ned was lying and pulled to a stop. She heard no sound except the whistling of the wind. Ned was absolutely silent, his eyes shut. He was as still as death.

Chapter

Five

NED LAY MOTIONLESS, one leg bent unnaturally beneath his body, his face frozen in a grimace of pain. Frantic, Nancy unsnapped her skis and dropped to her knees beside him. *"Ned,"* she called sharply. There was no response.

Nancy refused to consider her worst fear. She scooped up a handful of snow and rubbed it against Ned's face. Luke had brought her back to consciousness that way after the rope tow accident. Maybe it would help Ned.

She leaned over him, so close their faces almost touched, her ears straining for the sound of breathing. After a moment, she detected a faint groan.

"Ned!" Nancy was almost sobbing. Her eyes scanned his face for any sign of a response. To her relief, Ned's eyelids twitched and then opened slightly.

"Ned," Nancy called again. "Can you hear me?"

Ned's faint voice cut her off. "I must be dead . . . there's an angel rubbing noses with me."

"You clown!" Nancy scolded, relief washing over her.

"Going to kiss me to make it better?" Ned joked weakly.

The kiss that followed was anything but a joke. When Nancy drew back at last, she knew her heart was in her eyes. But her loving expression quickly turned to alarm as she watched Ned, his teeth gritted, slowly try to straighten his bent leg.

"Don't! Don't move at all until you're sure it's not broken!" Nancy gasped.

"I'm pretty sure it isn't," Ned said, wincing. "Have a look, will you?"

Nancy unfastened his boot and eased it off. Then she explored his leg carefully with her fingers, trying not to hurt him. "I think you're okay," she said finally.

"Good. Put my boot back on and help me get to my feet."

"No way! This leg is bad news—your ankle's already swelling."

"I've been hurt worse playing football."

All at once Nancy and Ned heard someone call to them from farther up the slope. George and Luke were silhouetted against the shining snow.

"Fantastic," Ned said. "They must have taken

the lift back up the mountain while we were skiing down."

"Come give us a hand!" Nancy shouted.

George swooped toward them, with Luke following close behind. "Everything all right?" she called. "We saw you—" Then she got a good look at Ned's leg, and whistled. "How did *that* happen?"

"I don't know," Ned replied. "One minute I was doing fine. The next, my boot was out of the ski and I was rolling down the mountain like an out-of-control snowball."

Luke bent down to check Ned's leg. "It looks like nothing's broken, but you could damage the ligaments seriously if you try to use it and you fall again. I'll ski down and get a carrier." Luke sped away.

"I don't need a carrier!" Ned shouted after him, but Luke was already too far off to hear.

"For Pete's sake, stop showing off about how brave you are," George scolded.

"Look who's trying to give lessons in good sense," Ned muttered.

George straightened up angrily. "What's that supposed to mean?"

Ned and Nancy exchanged glances. "Nothing," Ned said in a gentler tone. "I'm just furious with myself for falling. And I'm worried about how I may have messed up my leg for the baseball season. I'm sorry."

George looked dubious, but accepted the apology.

Soon after, Luke reappeared, pulling a stretcher behind him. Nancy and George helped him load Ned onto the stretcher. Luke laid Ned's skis, poles, and the boot Nancy had taken off next to him.

Then he strapped Ned in, picked up the stretcher's handles, and began a slow, careful snowplow down the treacherous slope. Nancy and George skied anxiously behind.

"Can't we stop for a rest?" Nancy called when they were halfway down. She could tell from Ned's face that, although Luke was trying to be gentle, the ride down was very painful.

"I know he's hurting," Luke said over his shoulder, continuing his snowplow, "but the sooner we get to the bottom, the better he'll feel." Nancy sighed. She knew Luke was right, so she and George skied on.

At last the foursome reached the bottom of the steep slope. Luke pulled the stretcher up to the doors of the first aid station. "Here we are," he said, unstrapping Ned and helping him to stand on his good leg. He supported most of Ned's weight as Ned limped into the infirmary.

When at last he was lying on a nice, motionless bed, Ned drew in a ragged breath. Luke looked at him with a faint smile. "You're a lot like me, aren't you? You don't like anybody to tell you what you can do or can't do. But let me give you one piece of advice, okay? *Don't* ski on a trail until you're ready for it."

"I know. But I have this daredevil girl-friend . . ." Ned gave Nancy a secret smile.

Suddenly Luke turned on Nancy, his face

darkening. "What? On the most dangerous slope we have? Are you crazy? If you want to take your own life in your hands like you did yesterday, that's one thing! But I *will not* allow you to go around here daring other people to kill themselves!"

"She *didn't*," Ned said with all the force he could muster. "The race was my idea."

"Was it?" Luke demanded harshly. "You don't strike me as the kind of guy who'd do something that stupid unless you had a pretty good reason. Maybe that reason was impressing Nancy Drew."

All at once Luke was shouting at Nancy. "You've got to be more careful! *Do you have any idea at all what it's like to be responsible for someone else's tragedy?*" He stopped, mid-breath, suddenly realizing that the others were staring at him. His eyes locked with George's.

George's face went from white to scarlet and back to white. With a choking sound, Luke wrenched around and ran out of the first-aid station.

There was a moment of stunned silence. Then George ran after him.

Ned managed a whistle. "Man, that guy's *weird!*"

"Something's weird all right," Nancy said, "and George knows it."

"What set Luke off like that, anyway?" Ned asked.

"I don't know." *Yet,* Nancy added to herself. "It sounds as if Luke was responsible for an accident. Maybe that's why he's such a dictator about safety." She frowned. "Although that doesn't explain everything." But before she could continue, the infirmary attendants came in.

After Ned's ankle had been examined and wrapped in an ice pack, one of the first-aid attendants drove Nancy and Ned back to Webb Cove Lodge. Luke and George were standing on the front porch of the lodge when the medical van arrived. They stepped aside as Nancy helped Ned up the steps. Clearly, they were embarrassed about what had happened in the infirmary, but didn't want to talk about it.

"I hope you're feeling a little better now," Luke said quietly as Ned and Nancy passed him.

George retrieved Ned's skis, boots, and poles from the van. "Thanks for bringing my friend home," she told the driver.

"Get better soon," the attendant called to Ned as he headed back toward Big Birch. Then the uncomfortable silence closed in on the foursome again.

The front door opened, and Liz's voice interrupted the awkward moment. "Lunch in five min—oh, no!" She stepped outside quickly. "What happened, Ned?"

"Bobcat Trail was too much for him," Luke said briefly. "He sprained his ankle."

Liz shot an alarmed look at Nancy. "Another accident?" she asked. Then she shook her head. "It doesn't matter right now, anyway. First thing we have to do is to get Ned inside where he can lie down." She looked at Nancy with concern. "You take it easy young lady. You look as though you've had the stuffing knocked out of you, too."

"I'm okay," Nancy replied, picking up Ned's borrowed ski boots and collecting the skis. She looked at them absently.

Then she looked at the skis again, hard, and dropped the boots with a thud.

"It wasn't the trail that caused Ned's fall," she burst out, "or our racing! The binding on this ski has come loose—one of the screws came out."

There was a chorus of shocked exclamations. Nancy cut through them sharply.

"Look at this!" She pointed. "This screw hole's a lot bigger than it ought to be. Somebody enlarged the hole so the screw wouldn't hold! This wasn't an accident—it was caused deliberately! And it nearly killed Ned!"

Chapter

Six

GIVE ME THAT!" Luke said sharply. He snatched the ski from Nancy's hand and examined the binding in silence. "This screw hole wasn't shaved down," he said finally. "It *wore* down. That's why the screw came out. It could happen at any time."

Luke seemed calmer, but his hands still trembled. He paused and inhaled deeply. "Ned, I'm terribly sorry. I haven't used these skis lately. I should have inspected them before I lent them to you."

"It's not your fault," Ned said after a moment. "Let's just forget it, all right?"

Nancy took the ski back from Luke. "It can happen at any time?" she asked skeptically. She wondered why Luke, who was such a fanatic about safety, *hadn't* inspected his equipment before lending it to somebody.

"On gear that gets hard use, yes." Luke stepped to Ned's side. "We'd better get you inside and lying down." He helped Ned hobble into the lodge and over to the couch in front of the fire. Nancy followed them, frowning and thinking that Luke was showing an awful lot of concern.

"It may be just a sprain—but if the swelling doesn't go down by morning, I'm going to drive you to the hospital to get an X ray," Liz told Ned. "I'll bring you an ice pack," she added, heading for the kitchen.

Nancy followed her. When they were alone, Nancy asked, "Liz, have you ever heard of a binding coming loose and leaving a hole like that?"

"It's possible. But it's definitely not common!" Liz's eyes narrowed. "You really think somebody deliberately tried to kill Ned? Who would have a motive for doing that?"

"You *have* had a prowler," Nancy pointed out. "Somebody looking in windows and writing MURDERER in the snow. None of that's very rational."

Nancy swallowed hard. Then suddenly she burst out, "Wait a minute! Those were *Luke's* skis!"

"Luke's skis," Liz repeated. "And he gave them to Ned." She paled. "Do you think he's to blame for Ned's accident?"

"An awful lot of accidents seem to happen around Luke," Nancy said thoughtfully. "These skis. The tow rope. It's just that . . ."

"What?" Liz demanded.

"Someone else could have seen Luke's skis and not realized that Ned would be using them. Same thing with the rope tow. The traps could have been set *for* Luke, not *by* him!" Frustrated, Nancy paced around the room. "I need a good motive, or even better, some useful evidence."

"This is really turning into a nightmare," Liz said, shuddering dramatically.

"Just stay calm," Nancy cautioned. "And let's keep this conversation between the two of us, okay?" She gave Liz's hand a squeeze and then hurried back out to Ned.

Nancy hadn't planned on a quiet afternoon with Ned, but she decided that the idea suited her just fine. However, they didn't spend it by the fire. With the aid of a pair of crutches that Liz kept on hand for such emergencies, Ned was able to limp out to the small lake beside the lodge. It was cleared for skating, and that's just what Nancy did. Ned sat and watched from a wooden bench, his leg propped up on a log.

Nancy was an excellent skater, and she found the rhythm of the sport soothing. She was glad to have a chance to mull over what had been happening. Writing didn't just appear in the snow, and bindings on skis didn't just wear down! As Luke well knows, Nancy told herself. Somebody had deliberately sabotaged those skis!

The problem was, who? And why? And who

was the intended victim? Liz had jumped to the conclusion that Luke had done it. Maybe he had, maybe not. Even if he hadn't, he apparently knew or suspected the answers to those questions. What exactly was he trying to cover up?

Much as Nancy loved solving mysteries, this one was causing some trouble.

She felt—lonely. The case had already come between her and George. And she could see it creating problems between her and Ned. Who's next? she wondered. Will Bess get angry at me? She skated over to sit with Ned for a while.

They returned to the lodge as the shadows started falling. Keeping his leg up all afternoon had done Ned's ankle good. The swelling had gone down a bit. As the aromas of chili and baking apples wafted into the lounge from the kitchen, the other guests began straggling in from the slopes.

Bess and Gunther appeared first. "We heard about your ankle, Ned. How are you feeling?" Bess said. "You missed some great skiing!" she called as she headed toward the dorm.

"You say that like a confirmed athlete!" Ned called back, grinning. Bess stuck her tongue out at him before disappearing. A group of college students appeared next and then, last of all, Luke and George.

Luke went directly upstairs without speaking to Nancy or Ned, but George came over to them right away. "How's the ankle?" she asked. Nancy noted that George's voice sounded strained.

"Hanging in there," Ned said lightly.

Nancy smiled at George. "How was the skiing?"

For a moment, George's eyes were radiant. "Oh, I had a great time!" she replied. Then her smile stiffened, and the light faded from her eyes. "Well, I'd better get ready for dinner." As she left the lounge, Nancy watched her thoughtfully.

Luke joined the guests for dinner that night, but he took a seat at the far end of the table near Liz. Ned hobbled over to the closer end, on his crutches, and Nancy, Bess, and Gunther joined him.

Soon, George returned. She had changed into dark red stretch pants and a Norwegian sweater, adding small gold earrings. She looked, Nancy thought, absolutely gorgeous. George hesitated for a moment, looking the table over, and then sat with Luke.

Luke didn't act like his usual aloof self at dinner. He actually relaxed and smiled, talking with George, the two of them in their own private world. They even joined the others after dinner, toasting marshmallows around the fire.

"How's the ankle doing?" Luke asked Ned.

"Pretty good. I guess it'll be okay by baseball season." He smiled and went on, trying to sound casual. "We've sure had a lot of accidents lately. Whatever happened to that old towline?"

"I threw it out," Luke replied shortly. He looked as if he was about to get up and leave, until he caught George's eye. "Not much skiing, I guess, where you come from?"

"Nope," Ned answered.

"How about *your* hometown, Luke?" Nancy put in. "Lots of skiing there?"

Luke's face tightened. He looked as if he was quite alarmed, but was trying not to appear so. "Little town in Maine," he said, and immediately turned back to Ned. "Do any competitive skiing?"

Ned shook his head. "If I had, would *this* have happened?" He laughed. "After this accident, I guess it's obvious that I'm no Olympic star."

Suddenly Luke seemed very, very uncomfortable. He tried to laugh with Ned, but the sound that came out of his throat was more like a croak. Nancy glanced at George and realized with a shock that George wasn't smiling, either.

Ned hit a nerve, Nancy thought. I'd better follow it up. "Is that something you'd like to do, Luke?" she asked. "Ski in the Olympics?"

"No," Luke replied shortly.

"Why not?" Nancy asked casually. "You're quite a skier."

"Luke's a pro." George cut Nancy off abruptly. "He wouldn't be eligible, remember?"

By now Gunther and Bess were looking at them strangely. Nancy signaled Bess with her eyes, and Bess jumped into the awkward pause with a giggle.

"What are we playing here, Twenty Questions?" she asked. Deliberately, she steered the conversation back to Nancy's line of questioning. "What competitive sports are you interested in?"

"I'm not. Competition can be destructive if

49

people care too much—or if they don't know what they're doing." Luke looked straight at Nancy. "You shouldn't go taking risks. Mountains have no mercy."

Nancy narrowed her eyes. "Some risks are worth taking . . . as long as they don't endanger other people."

Luke's fair skin flushed dark red. "One kind of sport I don't like is answering nosy questions. Excuse me." And with that, he stormed off.

As soon as he was out of the room, George jumped up. "For once in your life, can't you be something other than Nancy Drew, girl detective? Do you always have to go poking into people's private lives?"

"George—"

"Just forget it!" George cried. Then she stalked off after Luke.

Ned whistled. "I hope that risk was worth taking."

"It better be." Nancy's eyes followed George. "I hope I didn't hurt her too much."

"I'll see what I can find out," Bess said. She ran after George and Luke.

It wasn't until bedtime that Nancy met Bess in the dorm room and was able to ask her what had happened.

"Shh." Bess glanced significantly toward the door. "These walls are paper-thin," she whispered. "I could hear George and Luke from out in the hall, but all I could make out were a few words. Luke said, 'police,' and then 'investigation . . . broken leg.'"

"Broken leg." Nancy frowned. "They couldn't have been talking about Ned. I'm sure Luke broke his leg once, and badly, because of the stiffness in his one when he skis. But what do the police and an investigation have to do with that? . . . Wait—*broken leg!*" Nancy exclaimed suddenly. "Bess, have you ever heard of the Broken Leg Café?"

Bess just stared at Nancy. "The what?"

"'Haven't seen you since the Broken Leg Café'!" Nancy quoted. "That's what Luke said to the man who rescued me yesterday!"

Bess shook her head confusedly. "It doesn't make sense."

"We know one thing," Nancy said. "Luke talks to George in private about things he doesn't want the rest of us to hear."

At that moment, George walked in. She looked bemused, as though she'd just been kissed. But she did not look happy. She undressed and climbed into her bunk without a word. Bess and Nancy silently followed her example.

But long after all the others in the room were sleeping soundly, Nancy lay awake, arms locked behind her head, thinking. Finally she slid out from beneath the covers, put on her warm bathrobe, and tiptoed out to the lounge.

The fire had died down, but red embers still glowed in the darkness. Nancy lay down on the couch and stared at the coals, her thoughts tangled.

Suddenly she heard sounds overhead. A door opened somewhere, then closed. Footsteps quiet-

THE NANCY DREW FILES

ly approached the head of the stairs, then started down cautiously.

Nancy gripped the arm of the couch. Its high back would conceal her, but it also blocked her own view.

Someone, heard but unseen, was moving across the room toward the front door. The door creaked open and then there was silence. Nancy got up and crept to the window.

Moonlight, reflecting off the snow, showed a figure crouching on the porch. A small pool of light from a flashlight illuminated a pair of shiny skis. They were Luke's skis, the ones Ned had worn earlier.

The flashlight beam jerked upward for a fraction of a second, just long enough for Nancy to see the figure's face—Luke's face. He was checking out the skis he had insisted so emphatically had been *worn down*. And while looks might not kill, there was murder in his eyes.

Chapter

Seven

NANCY'S HEART SKIPPED a beat. What was Luke doing with those skis in the middle of the night? She had to know. Despite the fact that she was wearing only her bathrobe, she tiptoed to the door. Without a sound her fingers turned the knob. Then all at once, she yanked the door open.

Luke sprang up, the ski and the flashlight clattering to the porch floor. Even without the light, there was no mistaking the panic in Luke's eyes. He snatched the flashlight up again and shined it full in Nancy's face.

"You!" he hissed. "What are you doing sneaking around?"

"I could ask you the same thing," Nancy retorted. "I couldn't sleep, so I decided to sit by the fireplace for a while. The next thing I knew, somebody was prowling around out here. I thought I'd better check it out."

"You aren't afraid of anything, are you?" Luke said with grudging respect. He forced a soft laugh. "We must be having an insomnia epidemic around here. I couldn't sleep either, so I figured I might as well work on my skis."

"So why were you tiptoeing around out here like a thief?" Nancy asked.

"Look who's talking," Luke countered.

Nancy ignored his sarcasm. "Think you can fix them?"

"Why not? It takes more than a missing screw to ruin a good pair of racers."

Nancy sat down on the porch bench. "You don't mind if I watch you work, do you?"

Luke stood the ski back against the wall. "No. But I've changed my mind. The light's not good enough to work out here. And I don't want to wake the guests by working inside. By the way, don't go spreading around stories about your boyfriend's accident. You'll start a panic among the snow bunnies." Luke opened the door and pointedly waited for Nancy to go in first.

Nancy murmured a good night and went straight to the dorm. Whatever Luke was up to, he wasn't going to finish it that night.

Late as it had been when she fell asleep, Nancy woke very early. The other girls in the room were still sleeping soundly as she slipped on her black ski pants.

The sky was gray and the woods looked bleak

as Nancy let herself out onto the porch. The skis still leaned against the wall, exactly as Luke had placed them a few hours before. Nancy picked up the defective one and, holding the ski so that the early morning light hit it, examined it carefully.

Everything about the binding seemed normal except for the missing screw. The hole was definitely larger than the others, but now Nancy noticed something else, too. She could see knife marks, and traces of a grayish substance in the hole.

Nancy pulled her Swiss army knife from her coat pocket and pried some of the gray stuff out with her knife blade. She rolled it between her fingers. It was soft and malleable, like non-hardening putty or children's modeling clay.

And somebody, Nancy thought grimly, had deliberately put the clay there after enlarging the hole and then stuck the screw in it, so that it would pop out under the stress of skiing. Some accident! Just like my "accident"!

Nancy stood the skis carefully back in place and went inside. As she had hoped, Liz was now awake and working in the kitchen. Nancy greeted her, then turned immediately to the problem at hand.

"Liz, what happened to the rope Luke removed from the tow after I fell?" Nancy didn't mention that Luke had said he'd thrown it away.

"It's out back in the shed with the emergency generator," Liz replied. "You can go in if you want to. The door's unlocked."

The shed was a small building half hidden by a rise of ground. Nancy stepped in and flicked on the light. The generator was purring away quietly in a corner. On the floor were several large coils of rope. Then Nancy saw a smaller one. She could tell by the markings on it that it was the old rope from the tow.

Nancy felt all along the rope. At the end, her fingers stiffened. It had been cut three-quarters of the way through. The rest of the rope was frayed, as though a break had been carefully, maliciously arranged.

Suddenly a voice spoke from behind Nancy. "Don't you ever mind your own business?" It was Luke.

"Why did you lie to me about the rope?" Nancy demanded.

"Because Liz insisted we keep it, and it isn't safe to use! Now, listen, little Miss Detective—"

"Liz said I could come out here," Nancy cut in.

"Maybe she did. But *I'm* the one she'll hold responsible if any more accidents happen. This place is off limits to lodge guests." Luke took the rope from Nancy. Then, to her surprise, he smiled. "Anyway, breakfast's ready. Liz made apple pancakes with sour cream. And your boyfriend's looking for you."

It was so odd. Sometimes Nancy actually thought there was a nice guy underneath Luke's nasty exterior. She left the shed quickly and went in to breakfast. But she sneaked back afterward

—with Ned. She simply made sure that Luke wasn't around.

They went by a circuitous route, partly to find the easiest going for Ned's crutches, partly to avoid running into anyone. But when they reached the shed, Nancy stopped short in dismay. "Oh, *no!*" In the short time since she'd left before breakfast, the door had been padlocked.

"Now what?" Ned wanted to know.

Nancy laughed. "Easy. I'll pick the lock." Once again, she pulled out her Swiss army knife. She began removing the screws that held the door latch in place. "This wasn't here an hour and a half ago," she commented. "Luke must have installed it."

"Or Liz," Ned suggested softly. "Even if she did say it was okay to come and look."

Nancy nodded. "I know. I have only Liz's word about the prowler and the phone calls."

Ned blinked. "Do you really think Liz is behind all this?"

"Stranger things have happened. Maybe she'd cash in on a lot of insurance money if this place went out of business. Who knows?" Nancy remembered what Liz had said the day they arrived—that she was just a ski bum. "She seems so nervous sometimes. On the other hand, maybe she's just the hysterical type."

The door latch came off in Nancy's hand. Inside, the generator still hummed quietly, but the coils of rope were gone.

Nancy and Ned searched every corner, but

found nothing. At last they gave up. They left the shed, and Nancy screwed the door latch and padlock back in place.

"Okay," Nancy said as they headed for the lake, "it's pretty clear that none of these 'accidents' has been accidental. But the question is, why? I haven't come up with a good motive."

"I have," Ned said quietly. "Maybe someone is afraid of Nancy Drew, detective. Someone who, as the writing in the snow said, is a murderer. . . ."

Their eyes met. Nancy was more shaken than she wanted Ned to see. His theory was very possible. After all, the first "accident" had happened to her. Anyone could have heard Bess telling Liz that she was a sleuth.

Ned leaned toward Nancy. "Don't worry," he whispered against her hair. "Bad ankle or not, the next time anyone tries any funny business on you, I'll be there."

Nancy was shocked to discover how matter-of-factly they were both accepting that there would be a next time. But who would the victim be?

Nancy's troubled thoughts kept returning to Luke. He was so guarded about his past. And he'd lied about the damaged ski and the rope tow. Luke—was he the criminal or the target?

Face it, Nancy told herself. All I have so far is circumstantial evidence, but that evidence points to Luke Ericsen. Means, method, opportunity. I don't know what the motive is yet, but I'm sure all I have to do is dig deeper and I'll figure it out.

Then, with horror, Nancy realized something else. *George—one of my best friends—may have fallen in love with a murderer.*

Chapter

Eight

I'VE GOT TO warn George about Luke, whether she wants to hear it or not!" Nancy exclaimed.

Ned nodded. "Even if Luke isn't responsible for what's happened to us, he's definitely involved in some way. And we know he's hiding something."

"So's George! I'm sure of it," Nancy said apprehensively. "I've got to find out what it is. Otherwise I may never get to the bottom of what's going on around here."

Nancy's last words hung in the air ominously.

Ned looked at his watch. "You may still be able to catch her before she heads over to Big Birch."

Nancy caught her breath. "Can you make it back to the lodge alone?"

"Yes," Ned replied.

"Great!" And with that, Nancy took off running.

Nancy found George standing in front of the chair lift, snapped into her skis and ready to go. "Hey," Nancy said casually, "how about a race this morning?"

"Sorry, I'm busy now." George glanced at Luke, who was telling a few of the other guests about the schedule for ski lessons.

"George, I *have* to talk to you," said Nancy. "You've been avoiding me ever since we got here. I know it's because of Luke, and it makes me feel just awful."

"I never thought a guy would come between us," George admitted.

Nancy laid one mittened hand on George's arm. "I'm worried about you. Right now, I don't even know how to talk to you without hurting you. We've been friends for so long, but now you're a million miles away from me."

George sighed. "I'm just not sure I can trust you," she said. "You're saying all these horrible things about Luke, and you don't even know him!"

"Aren't you at least going to let me explain why? I think there are things you'd better know about Luke," Nancy said seriously.

George shot her a frightened glance. "Like what?"

"Like he may be connected with Ned's accident—and mine, too."

"Oh, come *on,* Nancy!" George exclaimed.

"George," Nancy pleaded, "you know something about Luke, and you've got to share it. Before someone else gets hurt."

"Listen, Nancy," said George quietly. "I've helped you on a lot of cases, but no way am I going to help you investigate *me!*"

Nancy paused to think. At last she said earnestly, "Look, if Luke's such a great guy, then convince me! Tell me what you know about him."

George's eyes dropped.

"You can't, can you?" Nancy persisted. "Because you know something about Luke's past, and it's not good."

"You don't know what you're talking about!" George cried.

"It has something to do with a place called the Broken Leg Café, doesn't it?"

Suddenly, uncharacteristically, George began to cry. With a burst of energy, she skied quickly away.

Nancy closed her eyes despairingly. What am I going to do with her? she thought. She resisted the temptation to run after George. She knew she'd blown it with her; she just hoped she hadn't blown the whole case, because now she was sure that one of her best friends was intimately involved!

Nancy walked slowly back to the lodge and found Ned alone in the lounge. "How did you make out?" he asked.

Nancy's shoulders sagged. "I couldn't have

done worse. George thinks I'm against Luke for no reason, and she's ready to defend him to her dying breath."

"Let's hope not literally," Ned said.

Nancy winced. "I did find out one thing, though," she added. "George jumped when I mentioned the Broken Leg Café."

"So you are getting somewhere." Ned limped over to Nancy and gave her a reassuring hug.

Nancy smiled. "You're not doing too badly with that ankle."

"It doesn't hurt much." Ned grinned. "If I stay off it today, I think I'll be able to ski tomorrow."

Nancy returned his hug. "So what are you going to do about skis? Liz says every pair is rented now."

"That's all taken care of," Ned replied smugly. "I phoned Big Birch and arranged to rent a pair there. We can drive over in the morning and pick them up. Maybe we should stop off at the Overlook Hotel while we're at it. I hear they've got a huge hot tub."

Bess and Gunther walked into the lounge just in time to hear Ned's last comment. "We're going dancing at the hotel tonight," Bess chimed in. "Why don't you come along? You'll have fun even if you can't dance."

Ned looked at Nancy. "You want to?"

"Sure! We deserve to have a little fun on this vacation!" Then Nancy's face became more serious. "Have you two seen George?"

Gunther and Bess nodded. "We just passed

her," Gunther said. "She was looking for Luke and she seemed very upset. Is something wrong?"

Nancy hesitated. "I had a talk with her about Luke. She thinks I'm picking on him."

"Oh." Gunther nodded. "I begin to understand. Our ski instructor is a bit of a mystery, yes? Perhaps not so good for your friend."

Before Nancy could ask Gunther what he meant, George herself walked in. She looked quite calm, though slightly red-eyed. "How's the ankle?" she asked Ned, obviously trying to act as though everything were normal.

Bess and Nancy exchanged glances. "We've just been talking about going to the Overlook tonight to do some dancing," Bess replied brightly. "Ned is much better. You and Luke want to come?"

George looked grateful. "Sounds good to me. I don't know what Luke's plans are, though."

"We can all ride over in my car," Nancy offered. At least that way everybody will be safe, she added mentally.

In order to keep an eye on Luke, Nancy took an advanced class with him that afternoon. He was a good teacher and an excellent skier, even if he did favor his right leg slightly. Nancy noticed that it didn't bend well at times. Had Luke damaged his leg in a skiing accident or some other kind of accident? Nancy wondered.

Luke did not show up at the lodge for dinner. Nancy preferred it that way, except that George looked so unhappy. Immediately after dinner, she scooped up a pile of ski magazines from the lounge and headed for the dorm.

Bess made an exasperated sound. "This has gone far enough. Come on," she said to Nancy. The girls went to the bunk room and cornered George. "Are you coming dancing with us?" Bess demanded.

George didn't look up. "I don't know. I told Luke you guys were going, but he wasn't too thrilled with the idea."

"Well, *you're* coming," Bess ordered. She pulled George to her feet. "You're already dressed for it, anyway," she commented, surveying George's tight gray pants and oversized turquoise sweater.

"If Luke wants to find you, he'll know where to look," she went on. "It's a good idea not to let guys think you're just sitting around waiting for them. Trust me." George allowed herself to be led out of the room.

The girls found Ned and Gunther and piled into Nancy's car for the two-mile drive to the Overlook Hotel.

The first sight of its ornate wrought-iron gates produced a squeal of delight from Bess. The hotel looked like a French château and was surrounded by trees decorated with little white lights.

The hotel's dance club was spacious and elegant. The band was playing a Stones classic, and the dance floor was already crowded. To one side, glass doors led to an indoor swimming pool complete with Jacuzzi.

Ned and Nancy found an unoccupied table as the others made their way to the dance floor. "This is a good spot to watch from," Nancy said. She smiled at Ned. "This is fun!"

Ned smiled back and took her hand. "You'd have more fun if you were dancing."

"We agreed you'd stay off the ankle today, remember?"

"That's no reason for you to stay off yours."

"I've done enough tearing around the mountain today. I'd rather sit the night out with you." Nancy meant it, but she found it hard to keep still while listening to the music.

After a while, Bess, Gunther, and George returned to the table. Gunther politely asked Nancy to dance.

"Go! I'll talk to George while you're gone," Ned whispered.

Nancy smiled and got up. Maybe George would listen to Ned more easily than to her. She followed Gunther to the dance floor and started moving to the bass beat.

Ned was right, it felt great to dance, even though the floor was crowded. It was impossible to avoid colliding with other people. Nancy felt her elbow connect with someone behind her. "Sorry!" she exclaimed, laughing, and turned around apologetically.

A deep voice said, "It's perfectly all right." She looked up at a tall, blond man with a deeply tanned face and vivid blue eyes. "I've already clobbered a few people that way myself," the young man said, smiling.

There was something oddly familiar about him, but Nancy couldn't quite place his face. "I really am sorry," she said again, turning back to Gunther.

"Are *you* all right?" the stranger's voice continued.

Those words! That voice! Nancy was sure she'd heard them before. She spun back around. The young man was looking at her with an odd expression in his eyes.

Nancy gasped. "It was you!"

Chapter

Nine

FOR A MOMENT Nancy and the blond man stood staring at each other. *"It was you!"* she cried. *"You're* the one who rescued me when the tow rope broke!"

The stranger's blue eyes crinkled into an admiring smile. "You must be quite a skier. You reacted so fast once you realized the danger, and you knew exactly how to fall."

"Not well enough to keep from getting knocked out!" Nancy laughed breathlessly. "I'm so glad to see you again! I was beginning to think I'd imagined you, and I never did get a chance to thank you."

"That doesn't matter. I didn't want to leave while you were out like that, but your boyfriend came up and took over. Pretty abruptly. Who is the guy, anyway?"

"Luke Ericsen," Nancy replied as the music ended. "And he isn't my boyfriend. Ned Nickerson is. Over there." She indicated the table where Ned was sitting. "Luke's the ski instructor at Webb Cove Lodge, where we're staying. This is my friend Gunther."

Gunther and the man shook hands, then Gunther excused himself and threaded his way through the crowd to Bess. You and Luke know each other, Nancy thought, looking at her rescuer. You were talking about being together at a Broken Leg Café. "I still don't know who *you* are," she said aloud.

"Michael Price," the young man introduced himself with another dazzling smile. "I'm a free-lance writer, mainly sports. Right now, I'm researching ski resorts in New England."

"I'm Nancy Drew."

"What do you do?" Michael asked.

Nancy decided not to tell Michael she was a detective. "Right now, I dance," she replied demurely. The crowd around them had started rocking to a new song, and Michael grinned.

"We do seem to be blocking traffic." Michael began moving to the music, and Nancy fell into sync with him. "Doesn't your boyfriend dance?" he asked.

"He loves to, but I won't let him tonight—he's banged up his ankle."

As Nancy told Michael about Ned's accident, he frowned and asked, "So this Luke lent him damaged skis?" He pursed his lips, thinking. "That sounds pretty irresponsible to me."

Nancy looked up into Michael's face. All of a sudden, she couldn't stand it anymore. Why was Michael pretending he didn't know Luke, when Nancy had heard them talking together? She *had* to find out from him what was going on!

"Michael!" Nancy exclaimed. "I'm going to be honest with you, and I hope you'll be honest with me. I don't trust Luke, and I need to find out more about him for the sake of a friend. I know you know him . . . so why don't you tell me whatever you know?"

A peculiar expression crossed Michael's face, but Nancy couldn't read it. Then he replied, "All right, I think I can be open with you. I said Luke sounded irresponsible to me. Well, there's more to it than just a hunch.

"You're right, I *have* met Luke before. He lent some equipment to someone I knew. And guess what—that guy had an accident, too. Only he wasn't as lucky as your boyfriend. He hit his head, went into a coma, and three days later, he was dead."

Nancy gasped. Luke really *could* be a murderer!

"Remember," Michael said, "I'm not telling you he did it on purpose. Maybe it was just carelessness. But that doesn't bring my friend back to life."

Suddenly the words Luke had shouted at her after Ned's accident reverberated through Nancy's head. "Do you have any idea at all what it's like to be responsible for someone else's tragedy?" he'd said.

Nancy shuddered. "How awful." George really may be in love with a murderer! she thought. And what can I do?

Suddenly, inspiration struck Nancy like a lightning bolt. It would be a whole lot easier to get George's mind off Luke if somebody else fell for her. Someone handsome and charming . . . "Why don't you come on back to our table and meet the rest of my friends?" Nancy suggested.

Michael shook his head. "Thanks, but I'd rather dance."

"I'd like you to meet George Fayne. She's a fantastic skier. She followed every minute of the last Olympic competitions on TV. I'll go get her. I really think you two have a lot in common."

Nancy started back to the table. This is great, she thought. Michael should be the perfect antidote to Luke.

Nancy found George and Ned alone at the table, both looking blue. Apparently Bess and Gunther were dancing again. Quickly, Nancy explained that she wanted to introduce George to a friend.

George studied Nancy for a moment. "I never thought I'd see you stoop so low as to fix me up with a blind date," she said. "Bess, yes, but not you, Nancy."

"Oh, come on. A blind date isn't stooping low! Don't make such a big deal out of it," Nancy said. "He's a nice guy."

"Look," George replied firmly, "I like Luke, even if you don't, and some good-looking, empty-headed skier isn't going to change that."

71

"He's not empty-headed," Nancy said. "Besides, this is more for him than for you. I think he's really lonely." So she'd lied. If her plan worked, that wouldn't matter.

"Oh, all right," George said, groaning, "but only because I know you won't leave me alone until I go with you."

But when the girls reached the spot where Nancy had left Michael Price, he was nowhere to be seen.

"Oh, well," Nancy said, "you can meet him some other time. Maybe he's just shy—like you," she added artfully.

Nancy and George went back to the table to find Bess and Gunther sitting with Ned and a few new acquaintances. Everyone was chattering about the various ski slopes, but Ned was unusually quiet.

Nancy put her hand over his. "Ankle bothering you?"

"It's fine," Ned said briefly.

Bess glanced from Nancy to Ned and back again. "If you guys are getting tired," she offered, "we can get a ride back to the lodge with somebody else."

There were immediate offers of rides from their new friends. "I don't want to drag Nancy away this early," Ned protested.

"I'd *like* to go. Really! We have things to talk about, anyway," Nancy said, thinking of Michael Price. "I'll go get the car and pick you up at the door."

"I think I can make it to the parking lot even if

I am a temporary cripple," Ned said with a laugh.

George shook her finger at Ned. "Look, super-jock, we all know you don't let sports injuries get you down. Just think of it as saving your ankle for the baseball season." She yawned. "I'm tired, too. I think I'll go home with you."

So Nancy didn't get a chance to discuss Michael with Ned as they drove home after all. But she definitely thought about him! How frustrating it was that he had disappeared before she'd gotten a chance to talk to him more.

He was my big chance to get information and clues, she told herself miserably as she lay in her bunk a little while later. And I let him slip away, trying to set him up with George. She looked over at her sleeping friend. Time to stop worrying about her and start solving this case.

Where did Michael fit in? Why had he been at the rope tow? Nancy felt a chill in spite of the thick comforter on her bed. *Could* Michael be the midnight prowler?

Nancy closed her eyes. Nothing made sense. But it will before I'm through, she swore. I'll track Michael down. And I'll find out why he and Luke pretended not to know each other. I'll get the answers—before somebody else gets killed on the slopes!

Chapter

Ten

WHEN NANCY WOKE up the next morning, George was already gone. "She had an early ski date with Luke," Bess said darkly. "I couldn't talk her out of it."

"We've got to get her to listen to us, and fast!" Nancy told Bess about her conversation with Michael Price, and Bess looked shocked. "Luke *could* have killed Michael's friend on purpose—but maybe he didn't," Nancy continued. "What matters is that his carelessness is causing dangerous accidents, so George's life could be on the line right this minute!"

"George is planning to help Luke give some of the ski lessons today," Bess told Nancy. "There are a lot of opportunities for accidents on the slopes, aren't there?" She rubbed her aching legs.

"Well, I guess Gunther and I had better sign up for those classes," she said bravely. "That way I can watch Luke and keep my eye on things for you."

Nancy nodded. "This is creepy, though, Bess. Michael might give Luke the benefit of the doubt, but after what happened to Ned and me, I wouldn't call what's going on here just coincidences. Three accidents, one of them fatal—and Luke involved in all of them. He's *got* to be doing it on purpose!"

Bess looked at Nancy, frowning. "But what's Luke's motive?"

"That's what I have to find out. Ned and I are going over to the hotel again today to look for Michael and to see if we hear anybody talking about Luke Ericsen. How long did Liz say he's been here? A few weeks? That's long enough for people to have started noticing anything odd."

As soon as breakfast was over, Nancy and Ned decided to head for the Overlook. But when Nancy turned the key in the ignition of her car, the engine wouldn't turn over.

"Maybe it's just too cold," Ned suggested.

"I don't know. It was colder last night than it is now, and the car was running fine then." Nancy tried the engine several more times but got no response.

"Want me to call a service station?" Ned asked.

Nancy shook her head. "Let me talk to Liz first."

When Nancy found Liz in the office and explained her predicament, Liz promptly took a key ring from a wall hook and tossed it to her. "Take Luke's old Jeep," she suggested. "He won't be using it until late this afternoon because of classes, and he leaves the keys here in case someone needs emergency transportation."

Nancy thanked Liz. "We'll take good care of it," she said. Then she and Ned were soon on their way.

At the Overlook, Nancy and Ned found the hotel's indoor swimming pool empty of swimmers, with no one around except a bored lifeguard. "We'll check the Jacuzzi out later," Nancy said with an enticing smile, "but right now, we've got work to do."

"How about this?" Ned suggested. "You check the hotel for Michael. I'll go spread my charm around the lobby and try to get the story on Luke. If he has such a bad reputation, then people should have something to say about him. We can meet in the coffee shop at noon."

"Okay," Nancy agreed. "Good luck."

Nancy started her search by asking for Michael at the front desk. He was registered, but the clerk wouldn't give Nancy his room number. She tried calling him on the house phone, but there was no answer. She checked the bar, the coffee shop, and the main dining room, all without success. Then she headed for the skating rink.

The rink, like the rest of the hotel, was plush. The roof was open to the icy sky, but walls of tinted glass held off the wind. There were lots of spectators, and Nancy guessed that many of the Overlook guests passed by just to watch.

She leaned against the rail and studied the skaters for a moment. With a start, she realized that one of them was Michael. An idea popped into her mind, and without a second thought, she rented a pair of skates herself.

Nancy laced them up, stepped onto the ice, and began a few warm-up tricks. She liked the music that was playing. It had a beautiful Latin beat to it. Gradually, Nancy added a few spins and easy jumps to her graceful movements.

Pretty soon a small group was watching Nancy and applauding. But all she saw was another skater at the far end of the rink—Michael Price.

As if feeling Nancy's eyes on him, Michael looked up. Then he bowed, his eyes glinting with mischief, and skated smoothly over to her.

"Shall we dance?" he inquired.

"Sure. How do you feel about talking after we skate?"

"What do you want to talk about?"

"Luke Ericsen."

"Okay," Michael said. "But I've already told you what I know about him."

Nancy had to admit that skating with Michael was great fun. He had a natural sense of grace and ease, and he knew a lot of tricks. But she was much more interested in getting some answers.

After a few minutes, she took Michael's hand and skated over to the railing. "So let's talk," she said.

"What do you want to know?" Michael asked.

"Well, for starters, why have you and Luke been pretending you don't know each other?"

Michael grimaced. "Quite frankly, after what happened with my friend, Luke and I can't stand the sight of each other. Neither one of us ever wants to see the other again, and I guess we both feel the less said, the better."

Nancy nodded. "Okay, I'll buy that. But there's something else. We've had a prowler around our lodge, a prowler who leaves some very frightening messages in the snow. . . . You wouldn't happen to know anything about that, would you?"

Michael coughed. "I—I don't know what you're talking about, Nancy."

There was a moment of awkward silence. Nancy could tell by the look in his eyes that Michael was lying. She understood why. Creeping around someone's yard in the middle of the night wasn't the kind of thing you'd want to own up to. What puzzled Nancy was why, if neither Luke nor Michael ever wanted to see each other again, Michael had gone to all the trouble of leaving that message. What did he hope to gain by it?

Nancy was beginning to get the feeling that Luke and Michael's history was just a bit more complicated than Michael was letting on.

Nancy saw Michael glance over her shoulder. "Speak of the devil," he said, "here's Luke now."

Luke marched up to the railing, his face grim. "You have some nerve helping yourself to my Jeep," he said tersely to Nancy. "It's meant for emergencies only. Coming over here doesn't count as one, so hand back the keys!"

"I don't have them," Nancy said hastily. "I left them with Ned. I think he's in the coffee shop."

"Fine. I'll get them. I do not want you driving the Jeep back to the lodge." Luke swung around.

"Just a minute," Michael called. An odd smile touched his mouth. "Luke—Ericsen, is it?"

Luke turned back and fixed his eyes on Michael. A peculiar expression was on his face. Hostile? Not exactly. It was more like . . . confusion, as if he were looking beyond Michael, seeing someone else.

Nancy felt confused as well. She had been certain that Michael and Luke already knew each other, but they were acting like virtual strangers.

"We used to have a mutual friend," Michael continued. "Dieter Mueller. Remember him?"

Luke just stood there, unmoving; but slowly, in a delayed reaction, his eyes began to bulge and his face went white. Nancy decided he looked completely terrified, as if he were watching his own funeral.

Then, all at once, Luke was running as fast as he could away from the skating rink, away from Michael—or from his own past?

As Nancy watched Luke racing across the snow, she turned to Michael—and found that his face had paled, too.

"You came over here in his Jeep? The old, beat-up one with the ripped top I saw parked out back in the lot?" he asked.

Nancy nodded. "We didn't realize he'd mind."

"I'm glad you won't be going back in it," Michael said. "And I'd advise you to stay away from anything else belonging to that guy. You saw what happened when your boyfriend used his skis!"

"Michael," Nancy asked bluntly, "who was Dieter Mueller?" She had to be sure.

For a minute, silence hung between them. "Can't you guess?" Michael said finally. "He was my friend, the one who borrowed Luke's skis."

"Michael, I'm sorry," Nancy said comfortingly.

"Yeah. Me, too," Michael replied. "Hey, are those people over there friends of yours?"

Nancy turned to see Bess and Gunther waving to her from across the rink. She and Michael skated over. "Where's George?" Nancy asked.

Bess shrugged. "She told me to get lost, in so many words. She's probably waiting for Luke back at the lodge. Or working off some emotion on the ski jumps!" She shook her head. "They had a date to go for a ride. Luke absolutely hit the roof when he found the Jeep was gone!"

Michael frowned. "That sounds very dangerous."

"Oh, George knows what she's doing where *sports* are concerned!" Bess said, laughing. "I think she could be an Olympic contender if she wanted to. Sometimes, I actually think she's going to go for it—she keeps such a close eye on all the tryouts.

"Besides," she went on with a grin, "if there *is*

any danger, she has the perfect bodyguard—Nancy Drew, the fabulous detective!"

Everybody laughed. But underneath the laughter Nancy felt a tenseness. The sensation lasted for only an instant. Almost immediately, Michael and Gunther were laughing at Bess's teasing. When Nancy looked at Michael, his eyes were warm with admiration. "I *thought* you were more than just a tourist! You're here on a case, aren't you?"

"No way!" Nancy exclaimed and laughed gaily. She managed to send Bess a warning glance as she went on smoothly. "I've ruined too many vacations that way."

Nancy glanced at her watch. It was just past noon. "Speaking of which, I'd better go find Ned. Now that I know where you're staying and you know where I am, let's keep in touch. Skating was fun. I'd really like to see you again."

Nancy's last comment was no lie. Michael was the only one around who seemed to know anything about her prime suspect. She *had* to see him again.

"You can bet you'll be seeing more of me," Michael said as Nancy stepped from the rink.

"He skates well," Gunther said, watching Michael glide across the ice as Nancy unlaced her skates and returned them. Then she, Bess, and Gunther headed for the coffee shop.

"What was going on out there?" Bess asked.

Nancy sighed. "I wish I knew. It was weird, though, that's for sure!" She turned to Bess and smiled wearily. "Listen, I'll have to explain all this another time. Right now, I think Ned and I need to be alone."

"Say no more," Bess replied promptly. "Gunther and I will make ourselves scarce."

"Thanks," Nancy said.

"Bye." Bess waved. "Take it easy."

Nancy found Ned drinking hot chocolate in a secluded booth in the back of the Overlook's coffee shop. "How are you doing?" he asked as she made her way toward him.

"I have definitely been better," Nancy said. She dropped into the seat across from him.

"Maybe we should forget this case," Ned said, a smile playing at the corners of his mouth, "and go on a ski vacation."

"That would be very funny if I weren't so upset," Nancy replied. She signaled to the waitress to bring her a hot chocolate, too. "By the way, did Luke get those car keys from you?"

Ned looked up, surprised. "No. I haven't seen him."

"I guess after what Michael said to him he was too angry to come and find you." Nancy quickly related the story to Ned.

"Wow, that's bizarre." Ned's face was serious when Nancy had finished.

"And Luke obviously feels very guilty about the accident," Nancy added.

"Yeah," Ned replied. "Michael really pushed a button in him, bringing the whole thing up like that.

"Oh, well. Since Luke didn't catch up with us, I guess we can take the Jeep home," Ned went on. "It would have been a real pain to walk all the way back to the lodge on this bum ankle—and I mean that literally."

The waitress brought Nancy her cocoa and she began to sip it slowly. "So, did you find out anything about Luke?" she asked.

Ned drained the last of his hot chocolate. "Not much. He's new to this area, just arrived during the past couple of months. Two college girls who work here part-time were definitely interested in him, but he wasn't interested in them.

"You know," he added, "whether the guy's a creep or a crackpot or a menace to society, I think he really does care for George."

"I don't know whether that makes the situation better or worse," Nancy said darkly.

"Anyway, the opinion of the athletes around here is that Luke's a very experienced skier. They say he's obviously had some serious racing training and that he's good enough to win medals in lower-ranked races—his bad leg would slow him down too much for the high-ranked ones. But he completely avoids all ski competitions, won't even watch them.

"Hey," Ned said suddenly, glancing out the coffee shop's large windows, "it looks like a storm is on the way. Maybe we ought to get going."

By the time Ned and Nancy had paid their bill and hurried out of the coffee shop, the sky was leaden, the air heavy and damp. Ned handed Nancy the keys to the Jeep, and she turned on the ignition. Soon they were speeding down the drive.

The approaching storm made the wrought-iron gates to the Overlook appear more ominous than glamorous. As the Jeep neared them, two enormous yellow snowplows came rumbling through, heading toward the hotel. Nancy had to jerk the Jeep to the right to avoid them.

"Close call," Ned commented.

"I know. I haven't got the hang of this thing yet."

They passed through the open gateway and out onto the mountain road. The wind whipped through the ripped canvas top. Wet snow began to drift down. "Hang on to your hat!" Ned shouted.

"What?" Nancy shouted back, her eyes intent upon the twisting road.

"I said—" The rest of Ned's words were lost in the roar of the wind.

Nancy shot a glance at him out of the corner of her eye. Then the steering wheel gave a convulsive jerk in her hands, and she turned her attention strictly to her driving. They whizzed around a loop in the twisting road, and she brought her right boot down on the brake.

It did not respond.

Was the road slippery? Or was it something worse? With a burning sensation in her throat, Nancy pumped the brake pedal again, negotiating a sharp curve as she did so. The pedal offered no resistance, and the Jeep didn't slow down even a fraction.

The brakes were gone!

Nancy yanked at the gearshift, trying to put the Jeep into a lower gear, but she couldn't manage to do it.

Ned poked her sharply. *"Slow down!"* he yelled.

"I'm trying to!" Nancy shouted back. The Jeep kept gaining speed. *"I can't stop this thing!"*

They careened around another curve, and suddenly the road dropped off sharply into a deep gully on the right side. On the left rose a cliff face, a wall of rock.

"Keep left!" Ned yelled, gesturing wildly. *"Stay by the rock wall."*

"I can't!" Nancy screamed. *"We'll be killed if there's a car coming toward us!"*

They roared around another bend, and the road disappeared into an impossibly tight hairpin turn. In front of them, the gully yawned, a bottomless empty space . . . and they were headed right for it!

"Jump!" Ned screamed. He tried to pull himself to his feet as the Jeep hurtled toward the gully beyond the curve.

In that instant, the one thought that leaped into Nancy's mind was of Ned's leg. It wasn't completely healed—he'd never make the jump. No way would she abandon him. She *had* to make that hairpin turn. Nancy gripped the steering wheel tightly and stuck to the road like glue.

Miraculously, she negotiated the turn. Then

she scrutinized the road ahead for any possibility of escaping their situation. All at once, Nancy saw her chance!

The road, for a very short stretch, opened out a bit, climbing uphill. There were trees on either side. And a fallen trunk lay against the cliff face.

Nancy could do one thing, and one thing only. She could try to slow the Jeep and get it under control on that short uphill stretch, then use the tree trunk to stop it completely—before it slammed into the rock wall beyond.

Deliberately, Nancy yanked the wheel left and sent the Jeep heading straight toward the granite cliff.

Chapter
Eleven

THE JEEP CATAPULTED toward the granite face of the cliff. As it shot ahead, Nancy yanked at the steering wheel with both hands. But her arms weren't quite strong enough.

Then Ned's hands closed over Nancy's with such strength that they crushed her fingers. Together, in unspoken agreement, they forced the Jeep to do her bidding, but they came so close to the cliff that the side of the vehicle scraped against the granite with an ear-piercing shriek.

The Jeep sped up the hill, slowing almost imperceptibly. Then it screeched up onto the fallen tree trunk, recoiled, tipped over, and came to rest on its left side at the edge of the road.

Nancy became aware of Ned's voice almost sobbing out her name. She was trapped inside the overturned vehicle, but Ned had somehow pulled himself loose. He was kneeling over her, brushing back her hair.

Nancy struggled to get her hand free. She locked it tightly with his. For several seconds they stayed like that, motionless, Nancy inside the Jeep, Ned outside. Then Ned spoke hoarsely. "If you hadn't tried that, we both would have been killed—"

"Let's not think about it. Please." Nancy shut her eyes.

Ned's fingers tightened on hers, but he spoke with deliberate calm. "We can't stay here. It's a bad curve. If a car comes around it fast, we could be in trouble again. How badly are you hurt?"

Nancy fought back an insane impulse to giggle. "It seems to me I've been through this before, after the rope tow broke," she murmured. She flexed her arms and legs, one at a time. "I'm all right. I'll probably be a mass of bruises tomorrow, but I landed on snow and nothing's broken."

"Then hold my hands and see if you can wriggle out." Ned braced himself against the fallen tree trunk.

Carefully, cautiously, Nancy twisted one way, then the other. It was like trying to get a cork out of a bottle. Slowly and painfully, she emerged. When she was finally free, she and Ned fell into each other's arms.

"I'm afraid we'll have to walk to shelter," Ned said finally. "It's starting to grow dark, and the storm's getting worse. We can't stay on this road!" He thought for a second. "We must have come more than halfway. Our best bet is to head for Webb Cove."

"You can't walk on that ankle—"

"If you're going to suggest that I let you go alone," Ned interrupted, "don't bother. Don't even think it! If I thought I was going to be able to ski today, surely I can take a short walk." Ned retrieved his crutches from where they had fallen in the road and he and Nancy, both still dazed, started slowly toward the lodge.

All at once Nancy began to laugh. Ned looked at her in alarm. "What are you giggling about? Are you sure you didn't break something in that beautiful head of yours?"

Nancy shook her head. "I was just thinking— if Luke looked murderous before, think what his face will be like when he finds out what we've done to his precious Jeep!"

"I'm thinking," Ned said grimly, "but I'm not laughing."

"I know," Nancy commented. "This time he's *really* going to kill us!" As soon as the words were out of her mouth, Nancy wished she could take them back. They'd come out sounding much more sinister than she'd meant. "Hey, what do you think, Ned? Could this be one more of Luke's planned 'accidents'?"

Ned groaned. "I bet you're right. Brakes don't usually just fail like that."

"And Luke's the most obvious person, isn't he? I mean, he's always involved somehow—his skis, his Jeep, the rope tow he was supposed to take care of— Wait, I hear something," Nancy exclaimed excitedly.

Behind them a motor sounded faintly. It grew louder, and then headlights swept around the curve. Nancy and Ned jumped out of the road, then started waving madly at the driver. The car slowed to a stop.

"Don't tell me you two tried to *walk*," Michael's voice said. Then he added in a shocked tone, "Was that *your* wreck I just passed? What happened?"

Nancy shook her head. "Something went wrong with the brakes." She shuddered.

"How did you get the thing to stop?" Michael asked gently.

"Nancy ran it up on a fallen tree," Ned said proudly. "If it weren't for that, neither one of us would be alive."

Michael frowned. "I thought Luke was going to take the Jeep back from you."

"He never found Ned," Nancy explained. "I think when you mentioned Dieter Mueller, he just got too upset to worry about it." She waited curiously for Michael's reaction.

Michael gave a short, mirthless laugh. "This is exactly the kind of thing I tried to warn you about, Nancy."

Ned's eyes narrowed. "Suppose you spell it out."

"Carelessness with his equipment—or dangerous jokes. Especially to get even with people who annoy him. People who take his wheels without asking, for instance."

"Some joke," Ned said.

Hmm, Nancy thought, something funny is going on here. Michael didn't mention dangerous pranks before. . . .

"Maybe it wasn't a joke," Michael said. He turned to Nancy. "Your friend said you're a detective. How much digging around into Ericsen's past have you been doing?"

"All I know is what you've told me," Nancy said evasively. "I certainly didn't come to Webb Cove to find Luke, if that's what you're suggesting. I came to ski."

Michael looked sternly at Nancy for a moment. Then he broke into a charming grin. "What I really should suggest is that you two get out of this wind before the snow gets any worse. Come on. Hop in the car and I'll drive you to the lodge."

"Fantastic," Nancy said gratefully, pushing Luke's "accidents" and Michael's changing story about them to the back of her mind.

"Thanks," Ned added as they piled into the car.

By the time they reached Webb Cove, the blizzard had begun in earnest—with the promise of much, much more snow to come.

Lights glowed from every window of the lodge as they approached it, and two cars loaded with luggage, skis, and people were pulling out.

Ned stepped out of the car slowly, wincing as

he put his weight on his bad ankle. "This is already beginning to swell up again," he said. "I'd better get off it." He leaned over and gave Nancy a kiss before hobbling inside.

Nancy eased herself out of the car. She had a lot of questions to ask Michael, but she didn't know how to put them into words. He was so nice and straightforward, yet she couldn't help but realize that there was something strange— and maybe a little ominous—about his relationship to Luke.

Michael got out of the car. "It's really beginning to come down, isn't it?" he said, flashing Nancy one of his heartwarming smiles and motioning to the whirling snow around them.

"Should mean good skiing," Nancy replied, grinning.

"Sure, when it stops in a few days and the sun comes out."

Nancy's grin vanished. "But until then, we'll probably be stuck here—snowed in. No one will be able to get in to us, and we won't be able to get out."

Nancy took a deep breath. "And the way you've been talking, it sounds like you think Luke is . . . insane. So before we get stuck in the lodge with him, I want you to stop hinting around about him and tell me straight!"

"I have no proof, Nancy, but I'm worried," Michael said soberly. "Maybe you and your friends should get out of here before the storm closes down the roads. You saw those people leaving just now. They've got sense.

"People from out of state usually think being in Vermont during a blizzard will be great. But if the power lines go down and you have no electricity—which also means no ski lifts—it's just awful."

"It seems crazy to leave a ski area in the middle of a huge snowstorm," Nancy commented.

"Well, why don't you talk to the others about it?" Michael said.

"I will," Nancy told him. "And why don't you come in and wait for a break in the snow before you drive back to the Overlook?" Michael smiled and followed Nancy inside.

The lodge was warm and cheerful. A huge fire roared up the chimney in the lounge, and as they entered, George and Luke came through the back door carrying armloads of logs.

"About time you brought my Jeep back," Luke said curtly. He noticed Michael. Nancy saw him swallow hard, then make the difficult decision to ignore him totally.

Michael raised an eyebrow. "They didn't—"

Nancy brought her heel down on Michael's toe. "We didn't mean to be so late," she finished smoothly. "Did we, Ned?"

Luke wasn't paying attention. He dropped his load of logs on the hearth and strode back out again without a word.

"George," Nancy said hastily, "this is the guy who rescued me when I fell, the one I wanted you to meet last night. Michael, meet George."

Michael came forward at once with his hand

out, smiling. "I hear we have a lot in common! Bess says you're practically an Olympic skier. I'd be glad to show you some of the trickier runs around here."

"No, thank you," George replied coolly. Her face had taken on a closed, shuttered look that Nancy knew only too well.

"Hey, give him a chance, George," Ned said easily. "We all know Luke's monopolizing your time, but—"

George shrugged. She turned to Michael. "I apologize for what my *friends* have tried to rope you into, but Luke told me what you said this afternoon, and I just don't think we'd get along very well."

"Hey, now, wait a minute!" Michael said quickly. "First of all, I don't get pushed into doing things I don't want to do. Second, I never could turn my back on a beautiful woman in trouble." His voice changed from flirty to serious. "You are, you know."

Something in Michael's voice stopped George cold. "Are what?" she asked suspiciously.

"Both. Beautiful and in trouble."

George's face went tight. "I don't want to hear this. If you'll excuse me, I'm going to go help Luke. We want to get the pre-blizzard chores done. There's supposed to be a lull in the storm this evening, and we plan to go night skiing at Lookout Ledge." She turned on her heel.

But Nancy wasn't about to let her friend run off that easily. She stepped in front of her and took her by the shoulders. "You are going to listen to me whether you want to or not," she said. "There's been another 'accident,' this time in Luke's Jeep!"

Quickly she described what had happened. Bess and Gunther arrived in the middle of her story and stood listening.

George's face went white. "Are you trying to tell me Luke's carelessness is responsible for almost killing you and Ned?"

"It might have been carelessness," Michael cut in. "It could have been planned. There have been too many 'accidents' around Luke lately."

George stared at Michael for a moment, her eyes beginning to blaze. "Apparently Nancy didn't tell you that I'm loyal to my friends!" she said fiercely. "And I don't pay attention to people who are prejudiced against them. So why don't you just take yourself back to your fancy hotel, Mr. Price! You've done enough to poison things around here!"

Michael gave Nancy a helpless shrug. "I tried," he said as he walked back out to his car.

George turned on the others, tears in her eyes. "I'm surprised at you, I really am! I thought you guys would have more faith in me."

Nancy felt frightened and helpless. George was determined to stick by Luke no matter how many people suspected him. What Nancy needed, she decided, was concrete proof, or George would never give him up.

"George, listen," Nancy said as persuasively as possible. "Even if the guy is a saint—don't go skiing with him tonight, not with a storm coming. He might be a good skier, but he does have a bad leg."

"Oh, come on!" George was indignant. "Why, in the last Olympic trials—" She suddenly stopped dead, as if she'd just bitten into an apple and discovered a worm in it. Then she turned and bolted toward the door.

Nancy's mind was churning. George had mentioned the Olympic trials. Had Luke been in them? If he had, then there were sure to be newspaper articles about him—and maybe even about poor Dieter Mueller's death.

There have got to be copies of old ski magazines in the public library in town, Nancy told herself. They just might hold the key to the Luke Ericsen mystery. All of a sudden, Nancy felt sure that she would crack the case soon!

But the question was, could she do it before the blizzard trapped her and her friends in the lodge with her prime suspect?

Chapter
Twelve

YOU'VE GOT AN important decision to make," Liz said to Nancy, Ned, Bess, and Gunther as they sat in front of the fireplace. "The blizzard has started. We have plenty of supplies and our own generator, but you could get snowed in here, perhaps for days. Are you going to stay or leave? All the other guests have checked out."

"What do you think we should do?" Nancy asked.

Liz spread her hands. "I don't like the idea of being snowed in alone with the prowler on the loose. On the other hand, I don't want you to be marooned here, too, out of a sense of duty."

"You won't like what I've got to say," Ned said, his face serious. "But I think we should leave—for George's sake."

Nancy shook her head. "You don't really think

97

George would come home with us now, do you? She'd insist on taking the bus home by herself at the end of the week, and staying here with Liz and Luke. We can't leave her."

Liz shook her head. "I feel sorry for that girl."

Nancy sucked in her breath. "Then you think Luke's guilty?"

Liz blushed. "Oh," she stammered, "I don't know. I—I guess if I really thought so, I would have fired him already. No, I feel the way George does—I want proof!"

"Against Luke?" Nancy asked.

"Yes! No . . . I mean, against whoever's guilty. It's the—the not knowing I can't stand!" Liz told her. "Anyway," she rushed on, "I think you should talk to George about leaving. The storm isn't supposed to get really bad until tomorrow, so you've got the evening to figure out what you want to do."

Dinner that night was strange with only six people at the long table. Luke had decided to skip the meal. George picked at her food, looking angry and miserable and doing her best to avoid talking to the others. At last Nancy broached the subject of leaving Webb Cove early.

"Are you kidding?" George exclaimed. "Leave Vermont in the middle of this gorgeous snowstorm? Miss all the great ski conditions? No way! You guys are crazy!"

"But, George—" Nancy began.

"Oh, no," George cut in. "If you want to go, then go ahead. I'm staying no matter what you decide."

Nothing any of the others said could convince George to change her mind. When the conversation turned to other subjects, she just moped again. She perked up, however, when Luke came in later. He and George spent the evening playing cards and laughing together while the others watched TV.

"At least she's here with the rest of us, instead of out skiing in the dark with Luke!" Nancy whispered to Ned.

During the evening, the electricity flickered several times. When it went out completely for a minute, Liz groaned. "That means the county power lines are in trouble. I'll have to go switch over to our generator."

Luke stood up promptly. "You stay put. George and I will do it." They pulled on their ski jackets and went out.

But they were gone fifteen, twenty, then thirty minutes. Nancy began to get worried. Murmuring an excuse, she sauntered toward the door. Ned followed. "You want to go find George?" he asked quietly.

"You know me too well," Nancy replied. "That's exactly what I want to do."

"My ankle's feeling better. Let's both go looking," Ned said promptly. They pulled on their jackets and, steeling themselves against the snow, plunged into the night.

Ned touched her shoulder. "Look." He pointed in the direction of the generator shed. A faint glow shone in the darkness.

Oblivious to the rapidly growing snowdrifts,

Nancy and Ned hurried toward the shed. Ned wiped some snow from a lower pane, and Nancy raised herself on tiptoe to look in.

George and Luke were sitting facing each other on a wooden bench, polishing their skis and talking earnestly. Or rather, Luke was talking, and George was listening.

All at once, George leaned forward to kiss him tenderly. In the next second they were locked in each other's arms. Nancy and Ned turned and made their way back to the lodge in silence, feeling a little embarrassed at having spied on them.

Later that night, as Nancy lay in the dark trying to sleep, she went over the strange collection of facts, rumors, and suspicions. They were like the pieces to a jigsaw puzzle. But somehow, when Nancy tried to put them all together, they just didn't fit. What was she missing?

Then Nancy had an odd thought. If Luke were the one causing all the 'accidents,' he'd done a great job of messing up his own belongings. Skis, a Jeep—they cost a lot of money. And he was making himself look awfully guilty. Would Luke really risk that just to get at Nancy and Ned? Maybe—if he really were insane.

Nancy stared into the darkness. The case seemed to revolve around Luke, but as possible killer—or intended victim? Had someone thought that Luke, not Nancy and Ned, would be using the Jeep and skis and rope tow? Then there was Liz. Nancy couldn't discount her suspicions about insurance money. And Liz seemed unnecessarily nervous at times.

Nancy shifted uncomfortably on the bed. Every time she looked at the case from a different angle, it came apart. If only she could get a line on Luke! At least she had another clue there—George's slip about the Olympic trials.

I've got to go to the library tomorrow, Nancy told herself, blizzard or no blizzard. If Luke was an Olympic hopeful, any scandal connected with him would show up in the ski magazines. That's where I'll find clues—I just have to!

By morning, the snow still hadn't stopped. Nancy decided to skip breakfast and go right to the library, before they got snowed in. She asked Liz if she could borrow her cross-country skis. With her car out of commission and the roads dangerous and icy, and especially after the "accident" the day before, Nancy thought she would be safer just skiing the two and a half miles to town.

By the time Nancy reached the library, the sky was white with snow and the wind was fierce. The library was deserted except for a middle-aged librarian standing behind the checkout desk. She looked up, frowning, as Nancy entered. "We're closing early because of the storm."

"There's something I have to find. It's urgent!" Nancy gasped, out of breath from her trek. "But I'll be quick. How long will you be here?"

"I'd better leave in ten minutes." The woman glanced worriedly out the window. "Can I help you?"

"I need information on the last Winter Olympics trials," Nancy said. "Magazine articles about accidents or scandals connected with it or with any of the competitors."

The librarian stared at Nancy. "You call that urgent?" she asked.

Nancy nodded. She didn't care if the librarian thought she was crazy. The woman disappeared into the back room and returned with several magazines. "You can't take these out. But you can have a few minutes to make copies, if you want." She pointed to the machine in a back corner.

Nancy ran rapidly through the tables of contents in the magazines. All covered the Olympics, and she put several aside to study later. Then she came to an issue of a skiing magazine with an article titled "Scandal on the Slopes."

Nancy began reading feverishly.

On the last night of the tryouts, the American bronze runner-up, Jon Berntsen, challenged a young German Olympic hopeful, Dieter Mueller, to a dangerous night race. It was a grudge match, fueled by an intense personal antipathy . . .

Nancy's heart leaped when she saw Dieter Mueller's name. But who was Jon Berntsen?

Suddenly the librarian was standing right beside Nancy. Nancy flushed and closed the magazine quickly. She'd been caught reading when she should have just photocopied the story and left. "Here's another article," the librarian was saying. "If you're going to copy anything, please do it fast."

"Thanks. And could you please reserve these for me? My name's Nancy Drew." Nancy hurried over to the photocopying machine. As she copied the scandal article, her eyes scanned the other periodical the librarian had produced.

It, too, dealt with the Mueller accident.

. . . both lost—Dieter Mueller, his life, in a fatal fall, and Jon Berntsen, the chance to become an Olympic winner. Berntsen's crash left him with leg injuries and a concussion. When he came to, Berntsen claimed to have amnesia, and no memory of anything just prior to the race.

However, sympathy for the young athlete quickly turned to suspicion when Mueller's bindings showed evidence of tampering. Berntsen disappeared before he could be charged, which has been generally regarded as proof of his guilt. Mueller's cousin, Gerhardt Mueller, also a member of the German ski team, vowed to make Berntsen pay for what he had done.

The librarian was putting on her coat and she looked impatient. "I'm ready to leave," she called.

Quickly Nancy copied the second article. As

she picked up the copies, she noticed a photo-
graph of the American ski team.

Berntsen. The name leaped out at her from the
caption. Third from left, last row. Nancy looked
intently, and her heart turned over.

It was a picture of Luke Ericsen!

Chapter

Thirteen

NANCY DIDN'T HAVE time to study either the original magazine picture or the copy she'd made of it. The librarian was at her elbow, visibly annoyed. "Young lady, please. We must close now!"

"I'm coming!" Nancy said hastily. She thrust the photocopies inside her jacket and hurried to the door. "I'm really sorry to have kept you, but it *was* important."

The librarian sighed. "It's all right, but now I hope you'll get back to your hotel as fast as you can. *Tourists!*" she added under her breath as Nancy passed her.

The wind was howling and whipping the snow into the air. Stores and businesses were closed in anticipation of the storm as Nancy skied through the center of town, her mind whirling.

According to Michael, Luke had loaned Mueller some defective ski equipment, which had caused the accident. But the magazine article said something completely different, that Luke—or Jon Berntsen—had challenged Mueller to a dangerous nighttime race which had resulted in his death.

Why had Michael changed the story? And why hadn't he called Luke by his real name? Was he trying to help Luke keep his awful secret? He certainly didn't act as if he wanted to do him any favors.

But even with her new information, one thing didn't change. Luke most likely was still guilty of manslaughter, if not murder! Could he have heard Bess mentioning that Nancy was a detective? That would explain those "accidents"—he'd be trying to get rid of Nancy and Ned so they wouldn't find out about his past.

But what about the letters in the snow? They made no sense. Unless . . . Nancy caught her breath. One of the articles had mentioned Dieter Mueller's vengeful cousin. Maybe *he* was after Luke (or Jon Berntsen). Maybe *he* was responsible for everything that had been going on at Webb Cove.

Nancy thought hard. Who around Webb Cove could be Mueller's relative? Michael? He was involved in the case somehow, and he certainly didn't like Luke. But he wasn't German.

Wait a minute, Nancy told herself sharply. *Gunther* is German. And he was at the lodge when the prowler episodes began. It would have been the easiest thing in the world for him to sneak out of the lodge at night and leave the message in the snow or damage the rope tow and the skis.

Nancy's jumbled thoughts began to take shape. Gunther had plenty of skiing know-how, from his experience on the German alpine rescue team. And he'd been cozying up to Bess since the very beginning, possibly to keep Nancy from suspecting him. He'd definitely put himself in a position where he found out much of what Nancy did or discovered. Nancy hadn't been very candid with Gunther, but Bess undoubtedly had.

Oh, great! Nancy thought, aghast. Either way, one of my best friends ends up falling for a killer. The only saving grace is that if Gunther is a Mueller, he'd have no reason to attack anyone but Luke.

Unless someone else became a threat!

Nancy reached the edge of the town and began cutting through the fields. Her eyes scanned the snow carefully, watching for obstacles. At the same time, her mind clicked along like a computer.

Luke as the target of a killer made more sense than Luke as a killer himself. Unfortunately, the killer was very reckless, and didn't care who else got caught in the traps he set.

The thought that Ned could have met Dieter Mueller's fate sent a shudder through Nancy. She stopped and leaned against a tree for a minute before going on. She was very conscious of how alone and unprotected she was there in the woods, in semidarkness.

The snow was whirling wildly, but through it, Nancy could make out a crossroads not far ahead. She had reached the bottom of Webb Cove Road. The slope would be murder to climb. She glanced around. Suddenly, she caught sight of a figure in a red-and-blue ski jacket some distance behind her. Whoever it was apparently hadn't seen her yet.

Acting on instinct, Nancy pulled herself behind a large fir tree and crouched down. She waited, concealed by the woods and the snow, as the figure approached and passed. It was Luke, also on cross-country skis. When he was a few yards past her, she cautiously pulled herself upright and began to follow him.

Luke made no attempt to ski along the road. He was heading toward the lodge, but by a circuitous route, one that was easier than heading straight up the hill. Luke reached the crest of the last rise before the lodge and then disappeared behind the hill. Panting, Nancy reached the top a few moments later. She skied down the incline after Luke.

He was not heading for the lodge after all, she realized then, but toward the shed that housed Liz's electric generator. What's he up to? Nancy asked herself, frowning.

She decided on a bold move. Giving him just time enough to get inside but not, she hoped, time to lock the door, she skied straight to the building.

She was in luck. The door was not locked, and she pushed it open. Luke was bent over the generator, and as he felt the rush of cold air he straightened quickly. "What are *you* doing here?" he demanded.

"I was just about to ask you the same thing."

"I went to town to get parts for Liz's shortwave radio, if you must know," Luke said coldly. "It's not working right, and we'll need it if the telephone lines go down. And since there's a major blizzard in progress, it did occur to me to check the generator to make sure it's working properly! What were *you* sneaking around the woods for?"

"I went to the library to get some books to read," Nancy said primly.

Luke gave a harsh laugh. "Well, you can't read them here! Go back to the lodge and curl up by the fire with your boyfriend. You'll get yourself in a lot less trouble that way!" He waited pointedly for her to leave, then followed, locking the shed door behind them. "And don't come back here."

Luke didn't accompany her in the direction of the lodge, but took off as soon as he had snapped on his skis. He went by a path Nancy had not noticed before. After giving him a few moments' head start, Nancy followed.

She kept her eyes glued to Luke. Where was he going in the middle of the storm, anyway? Nancy couldn't tell where the path was leading. But she did see something else.

Barely visible in the thickening blizzard was a rope strung across the trail at neck height. Anyone skiing quickly down that path would be caught right across the throat. Nancy watched in horror as Luke headed toward it. He was skiing swiftly into a death trap!

Chapter

Fourteen

"LOOK OUT!" Nancy screamed. *"Luke!"*

Luke reacted an instant too late. He carved a tight turn and tried to brake, but the rope caught him squarely across the forehead and he was thrown to the ground. At least he wasn't badly hurt. Immediately, he pulled himself up to a sitting position and groaned, rubbing his head.

"Are you all right?" Nancy called, skiing over and kneeling beside him. He nodded vaguely.

"Don't try to talk." Nancy pulled off his cap. She noticed that it was actually a blue-and-white ski mask with the lower part rolled into a cuff. "If you'd kept this pulled down over your face, you'd have made out better," Nancy said, looking at the broad rope burn Luke had received above the eyebrows.

"What hit me, anyway?" Luke muttered.

"There's a rope strung across the path. If you hadn't ducked, it would have caught you right across the throat." Nancy squinted down the path. "Where does this trail lead, anyway?"

"To Liz's storage shed. I needed to get some storm supplies."

"Who knew you were coming here?" Nancy demanded.

"I don't know. Nobody. Anybody." Luke pulled himself to his feet. "Liz and I are the only ones who use this trail."

"Luke, who's trying to harm you?" Nancy asked gently. "Please tell me. I can help."

Luke turned and looked straight at her, his face deeply troubled. "There's only one way you can help. Clear out! All of you! Before the blizzard shuts you in!"

"*All* of us? Including George?"

"Especially George! She's terrific, and I don't want her getting hurt!" Abruptly, Luke turned and pushed off into the woods.

Nancy headed for the lodge, thinking hard. *Now I know where Luke fits in—as prospective victim. And he knows who's trying to kill him,* she decided, *but he's been trying to keep me from finding out because then he'd have to tell me the whole story. Luke doesn't want anyone to know he's Berntsen, because Dieter Mueller's suspicious death is still hanging over his head!*

That was the only logical explanation for the way Luke had been acting—and the way George

112

had been acting, too. George must have recognized Luke as Jon Berntsen from all the Olympic coverage she'd watched on TV! It was just like George to protect and defend him, if she believed he'd been accused unjustly of Dieter Mueller's death.

But someone else at Webb Cove didn't believe that accusation was unjust. That person could be Dieter Mueller's good friend, Michael Price. Or he could be a relative of Dieter Mueller—Gunther?

When Nancy reached the lodge she leaned her skis against the porch wall and hurried into the lounge without even taking off her jacket. Everything in the lodge seemed incongruously calm. A fire burned as always, Ned and George were playing Monopoly, and Gunther and Bess were snuggling by the fire. They all turned and looked at Nancy as she entered.

"You look like you've seen a ghost, Nancy!" Bess said, giggling at her snow-covered friend. "In fact, you look like a ghost yourself!"

"We almost *did* have a ghost," Nancy said bluntly. "Luke almost got killed."

George gasped and immediately started for the door.

"Sit down!" Nancy said firmly. "He's all right, and he's gone off somewhere. Besides, for your own protection, he doesn't want you with him." She turned to Ned. "We need to talk. Alone. Now."

"But what happened to Luke?" George cried.

"I'll tell you the whole story later," Nancy replied, taking Ned's hand and leading him toward the kitchen.

Nancy pulled up two chairs and, in a low voice, told him about her morning and her suspicion about Gunther.

"Here." Nancy pulled the two articles out of her jacket. "Read these."

"Luke's Berntsen, all right," Ned said when he'd finished reading and had examined the picture. "If Gunther *is* out to get him, I don't want George caught in the cross fire."

"Me neither," Nancy said. "But we can't get George to leave."

"Look," Ned said, "I'll try to convince her to go. Maybe she'll listen to me."

"It's worth a try," Nancy said.

They went back to the lounge and found that Gunther was gone. I hope Luke's keeping his eyes open for trouble, Nancy thought anxiously, but there was nothing she could do to help him.

Ned immediately took George off alone. When they came back, she said to the others, "You guys go pack. I," she added defiantly, "am going to tell Luke we're leaving, even if I have to ski this whole mountain range to do it!"

Nancy and Bess headed for the bunk room and started throwing their clothes quickly into their bags. We'll head straight for the police, Nancy thought. I bet we can wrap up the case in no time flat.

"It's too bad we're leaving early," Bess said,

"but I won't mind so much if Gunther decides to come with us."

Nancy looked at her friend sympathetically. "I don't know how to tell you this, Bess," she said, "but I don't think he will." She gave a rapid summary of her suspicions about Gunther. "If he's the one who's after Luke, I'm sure he'll stay for the storm and try to finish him off. And if that's so, I just hope we can get the police out here before that happens."

Bess's face was flushed. "Gunther isn't out to kill Luke," she said steadily. "I *know* him."

"We've all been fooled by people who seemed nice," Nancy said.

Bess frowned at her. "Think what you want, but you'll find out you're wrong. Anyway, the thing that matters most is getting out of here. After all, somebody around here is a potential killer, and I don't want to be around if and when he succeeds. Come on, let's finish packing. I'll get George's stuff for her."

Within an hour they were loading Nancy's car. Ned got the battery recharged, so there were no start-up problems. The power lines were down and Liz was using candles, firewood, and the generator out back to run the lodge. Gunther, as Nancy had predicted, had decided to stay on. George was close-mouthed and somber, standing mournfully beside Luke.

The snow was coming down much harder. The lodge looked like something from a dark fairy tale, with lights burning only in the windows of the lounge. For a moment, that picture crystallized in Nancy's mind—the dark lodge; Luke deeply anxious and frightened; George, also frightened but defiant; Liz trying to be strong.

Then the image was broken by a voice calling cheerfully, "Hey, there."

It was Michael Price on cross-country skis, coming from the direction of the Overlook and carrying a loaded backpack. "Where are you people going?" he asked.

"Someplace safe," Luke replied stiffly. "Why are you here?"

Michael stared at Luke for a moment with a decidedly unfriendly air. Then he turned to Nancy. "I'm sorry you waited so long to leave. There's no point in trying to get out now. I heard at the hotel that the fallen power lines have blocked the roads to the highway. That's why I'm here—I brought you some supplies." He pointed to his backpack.

"We have enough, but thanks for the thought," Liz said quietly. "Why don't you all come back in?"

Michael set his backpack on the porch and helped Luke unload the luggage from the car. Suddenly Luke turned angrily away.

"I'm going to ski over to the hotel to see if I can get a two-way radio from somebody there," he said. "Ours is out of commission. I can't get it to work at all."

"Wait, Luke. I'll go with you," George cried.

Luke turned, a gentle smile lighting his face as he looked at George. "No," he told her. "You stay here for now. But I'll meet you up at Lookout Ledge at nine o'clock, okay?" He turned to Michael. "I hope you're gone by the time I get back." With that, he stalked away.

"There's that temper," Michael said to Nancy, shaking his head. "See what I mean?"

But George overheard the comment. "If Luke's furious, you made him that way," she snapped.

"Now, wait a minute—"

"No! You wait! I know exactly what you're up to, and I think you're disgusting! You're deliberately loading a guilt trip on him—" George broke off, her eyes blazing, and stormed into the lodge.

"What did I do?" Michael asked.

"You set that up," Nancy answered absently. But her mind was on other things. In a way, she decided, she was glad they were staying on at the lodge. Now she would have to solve the mystery herself.

The rest of the time before dinner passed uncomfortably. Bess remembered that she had a small pocket radio somewhere in her luggage, and she dug it out. It produced mostly static, but provided a much-needed distraction.

Gunther asked her to dance to some barely audible rock music. From a news bulletin on the radio, they heard that, although the snow had stopped momentarily, the worst of the blizzard was yet to hit.

At last Liz brought in a huge pot of stew and set it on the table. "Dinner!" she announced.

Bess left to get George but came back to report that George wasn't eating.

"Oh, yes, she is," Liz said grimly. "I'm sick and tired of all the emotional carrying on around here!" She stalked off in the direction of the dorm and reappeared with an angry-looking George in tow.

"I'd better beat the second onslaught of the storm," Michael said. "Wish I could stay for dinner, but I don't think it's such a great idea."

"Thanks for the provisions. I hope you get home safely," Liz said.

The others, except for George, said good-bye, and then they all sat down to dinner. They were just finishing when the old wall clock began chiming the half-hour—eight-thirty.

George rose from the table and strode to the door. "I'm going to meet Luke at the ledge," she said, as if daring her friends to try to stop her. She quickly put on her outdoor clothes, then stepped out into the storm.

Nancy stood up. "I'm going to follow her."

Ned rose too. "I'll go with you."

"What about your ankle?" Nancy asked.

"It'll hold me. If you're going, I'm going."

"Okay. Bess and Gunther, you stay here," Nancy said. The last thing she needed was Gunther out at Lookout Ledge with Luke in the darkness. "Liz," she continued, "we'll need directions to the ledge."

"No problem," Liz said.

A few minutes later, Ned and Nancy were pulling on their heavy outdoor clothing. Once outside, they stepped into cross-country skis. Nancy stood for a moment, looking out into the dark forest. How still the night seemed. Every sound was strangely muffled by the falling snow.

Nancy shuddered. Somewhere in the silent night a killer lurked.

Ned reached out and squeezed Nancy's hand.

"I'm so glad you came!" she whispered.

"I would never have let you go out on this one alone," Ned said. He kissed her softly, and they started off toward the ledge, searching the hillsides for some sign of George or Luke.

But when Nancy and Ned reached the ledge, there was no sign of them. "Where are they?" Nancy asked anxiously. She glanced at her watch. "It's ten after nine."

"Maybe they've already met and have gone off together," suggested Ned.

"Could be," Nancy replied. "With this snow coming down, there's no way to tell whether there were tracks here ten minutes ago. Or else—" Nancy's words were cut off by a scream. "It's George!" she cried.

Nancy and Ned stood silently, listening. It was hard to tell which direction the scream had come from. The snow muffled and distorted all sounds.

Ned gripped Nancy's arm. "I could swear it came from right over there, through that clump of trees," he whispered.

Then it came again, a loud, desperate scream, and the sounds of a struggle.

Nancy pushed off, skiing with all her strength and speed. Ned was right behind her. They burst

119

into a clearing and jerked to a stop, horror-struck.

On a narrow ledge, two figures were locked in a death struggle. George had been forced into a kneeling position on the cliff edge. Her back was arched and her hands scrabbled desperately to pull a masked figure's hands from around her throat. But that blue-and-white ski mask was distinctive—it was Luke Ericsen's!

Chapter

Fifteen

GEORGE STRUGGLED WITH all her might, but the attacker—Luke?—was too strong. Luckily, at that moment, Ned shot forward. He grabbed Luke's arms from behind, wrestling him backward. At the same time, Nancy flung herself across George's legs and hung on. They were so near the edge of the cliff that one false move could send them over.

In the split second that Luke was thrown off-guard, George's hands grabbed his wrists and jerked them up and out. His hold broke and George fell backward, saved from the cliff edge only by Nancy's grip.

Ned battled Luke, throwing a punch into his masked face that rocked him back on his skis. Luke snatched up his ski pole and sent it whistling toward Ned's head, but Ned blocked it, moving in for another punch. Suddenly, Luke kicked out viciously, his ski slamming into Ned's injured ankle. As Ned fell, he tried to tackle Luke.

Nancy looked up just in time to see Luke deftly sidestep Ned, then sweep up his other ski pole. Pushing off with his right leg, then his left, he vanished from sight around a curve in the path.

For a moment everyone remained frozen with shock. Then Ned scrambled to his feet and started after Luke.

"Not now!" Nancy shouted. "We can get him later!" George needed them more. She was gasping for breath and sobbing as Nancy held her in a warm hug. There were bruises across her throat, and her hat and scarf were gone, pulled off in the struggle. *And Luke never even lost his ski mask,* Nancy thought with anger.

"Don't try to talk," she murmured as George struggled to make herself understood. "Does anything feel as if it's been torn or broken?" George shook her head. Clearly she was hurt, but it didn't seem as if anything serious was wrong.

"What happened?" Ned asked.

"I don't know," George whispered.

Nancy and Ned exchanged glances. They had never seen George so shaken before. It was going to be a while before she could begin to explain anything. "It's all right . . . it's all right," Nancy soothed her. "You're safe now." She only hoped she sounded more convinced of that than she felt. They had scared Luke off, but there was no knowing what he would do next.

What mattered was getting George back to the lodge. "Can you walk?" Ned asked.

George nodded and started to pull herself to a standing position. Then her eyes, staring past the others, grew wide with fear. Nancy and Ned turned in the direction of her gaze.

A figure on skis had come soundlessly around the curve—a figure in a too familiar red-and-blue ski jacket and a ski mask rolled up into a cap. Luke had come back. He stopped short, looking at them blankly.

"What's going on?" Luke's face changed as George turned away from him, and he caught sight of her bruised neck. *"George, are you hurt?"* He started forward. George shrank away with a cry and Ned shot forward to fend Luke off.

"That's a strange question," Nancy said, just barely controlling her fury.

Luke's eyes snapped from one figure to another. "What's happened? George, why didn't you show up at the hotel?"

Nancy stared at Luke, "What do you mean, at the hotel? You told her to meet you at Lookout Ledge. We all heard you!"

"Yes, but when I was at the h-hotel t-trying to borrow a shortwave radio," Luke stammered, "the clerk said she had a message for me. She said George Fayne had called to say I should meet her at the hotel."

He turned to George. "I waited and waited.

123

Finally I got worried and came looking for you. Now, will somebody *please* tell me what's happened?"

"You creep!" Ned burst out. "You *know* what happened. You just tried to strangle George and throw her over the ledge!"

Luke's jaw dropped. "How can you say that?" he cried. "I wasn't here! It wasn't me! And I swear, I'll kill whoever tried to hurt you!"

He reached out and touched her gently. George jerked away, trembling violently.

Nancy studied Luke's strained face. If Luke was acting, he was doing it very well. She turned to George. "Did you ever see your attacker's face? Was he wearing the ski mask the whole time?"

George shivered. "I—can't remember."

"George, it wasn't me!" Luke cried. He gave her an aching look. She didn't answer, and he turned to Nancy. "Is she hurt? We've got to get her back to the lodge."

"We'll take care of that," Ned said tightly. "You get lost."

"Tell me one thing. The attacker—which way did he go?" Ned jerked his head down the trail. Luke gave George one last troubled glance and then, without a word, skied off in the direction Ned had indicated.

Nancy watched him, noticing again that he skied with most of his weight on his good left leg, dragging his right one a bit. Suddenly, it hit her. How could this be the same man who'd hurried away moments before? With his injured right leg,

Luke would never have been able to push off the way the other had!

But who else could it have been? The mysterious man had worn the same mask and the same jacket as Luke. Nancy didn't know the answer to her question, but she knew that she'd have to wait until later to figure it out. They had to get George back to the lodge.

"George, let's go home," Nancy said gently.

Back at the lodge, Nancy and Bess helped George into bed. Then Nancy locked the door and said, kindly but firmly, "Okay, George, now talk. You know you need to, and it's important."

"I . . . I just don't know what to say!" Tears welled in George's eyes. "I met Luke where we were supposed to. He didn't say anything, just motioned for me to follow him. It was like . . . like he wanted to show me someplace really special. I was really happy, you know? And then—then we got to that ledge—" She broke off, sobbing.

"What did he do?" Nancy asked calmly.

"He just came after me, and grabbed me."

"Like somebody straight out of one of those cheap horror movies!" Bess exclaimed. "Why on earth would Luke do that to George?"

"It wasn't Luke. I could tell from the way he skied," Nancy said abruptly, searching George's face for a reaction. Even though she thought Luke had betrayed her, George was still holding back information.

Nancy took hold of George's hands. "It wasn't

Luke," she repeated more gently. "Or should I say, it wasn't Jon Berntsen?"

George gasped. "How long have you known?"

"Just since this morning."

George drew in a ragged breath. "And I thought I was being so smart, hiding the *Sports Illustrated*s that told about the scandal. I guess Liz never read them, or she'd have known, too."

Maybe she did read them, Nancy thought.

"Will somebody," Bess asked plaintively, "please tell me what's going on? Who's Jon Berntsen?"

Nancy explained the scandal to her. Bess's eyes grew very dark. "Then Luke *is* a killer!"

"No, he's not!" George cried passionately. She gripped Nancy's hands. "Luke didn't kill Dieter Mueller! I know he didn't! No one has treated him fairly."

"George, has Luke admitted to you that he's Berntsen?" Nancy asked.

George nodded. "But I'd already guessed. His face was familiar—and then when I saw his skiing style, I knew for sure."

"Does *he* say he was responsible for Dieter Mueller's death?" Nancy probed.

"He's sure he wasn't. At least, he *says* he's sure. But he can't remember anything that happened right before and right after the race."

Nancy could see the pain and exhaustion in George's eyes. "Don't think about it now. Things will look better in the morning," she said soothingly.

She sat holding her friend's hand until George fell asleep. When her breathing had settled into a steady rhythm, Nancy slipped away from the bed.

All she wanted was a nice, long shower to wash the day's terrible events away.

But Bess had other things on her mind. "Nancy, I've got to talk to you," she whispered urgently.

Nancy realized that Bess had looked troubled ever since she and Ned had brought George back.

"It's about Gunther," Bess said shakily. "I—I don't know how to say this, and I didn't want to say anything in front of George because she's so upset, but . . . well, it's just that as soon as you and Ned went out to find George, Gunther left, too. He didn't say where he was going, but I saw him putting on his cross-country skis."

Nancy gasped. "If he skied really fast—and we know he can—then he could have gotten to George before we did and . . ."

Bess let out a little cry. "Nancy, what are we going to do?"

Nancy wrapped her arms around Bess. "We can't let on that we know," she told her, "not until we have proof that we can take to the police—and until we're no longer stranded with him!"

"I don't think I can do that," Bess said in a small voice.

"You have to," Nancy told her earnestly, "no matter what it takes. Now I'm going to tell Liz and Ned what we know about Luke. Then I hope we can sleep. We're going to need a lot of rest if we're going to make it through tomorrow alive!"

By morning, conditions at the lodge had worsened. The girls awoke to bitter cold. When they entered the lounge, they found Ned and Gunther helping Liz cook breakfast in the fireplace.

"Bad news," she announced. "The generator's failed—and it looks like someone may have tampered with it. We've got no lights, no stove, no heat, and no running water. Luke's already skiing to the Overlook to get help."

Suddenly there was a startlingly loud pounding at the door. "That can't be Luke back already," Liz said as she went to open it.

Michael stamped in, bundled up against the storm. "I skied over from my hotel to see how you're doing. When I saw that there weren't any lights on, I got worried!"

"Somebody sabotaged the generator," Ned said grimly.

Michael stared at him. "You're kidding!" Then he added, "You realize it must have been Luke who did it."

Suddenly Nancy had an idea. "You should see the stories I found at the library about the last Winter Olympics trials!" she said. "They were all about Jon Berntsen and Dieter Mueller."

"Dieter Mueller!" Gunther exclaimed. "What does he have to do with all this?"

"Did you know him?" Nancy demanded.

Gunther nodded. "We were on the same junior

racing team when we were quite young. What happened to him was tragic—but, of course, he shouldn't have taken a wild dare like that in the first place. I don't know Jon Berntsen, though."

"Do you know either of them?" Nancy continued, turning to Michael.

Michael's eyes were guarded and he looked at Nancy strangely. "You know . . ."

Then George exploded into a torrent of words. "Oh, we know all right! You know who he is! You've been baiting him, poisoning people's minds, implying horrible things. . . . Luke wouldn't be in the mess he's in right now if it weren't for you!"

But Liz cut her off. She was listening to something outside the window. "That's funny," she said, "I hear thunder on the mountain. That usually doesn't happen during a snowstorm."

A moment later, the sound came again. The lodge shook with vibrations, and coffee cup fell off the table. "That's not thunder!" Liz exclaimed.

Everyone threw on ski jackets and hurried outside. About a mile down the road, a cascade of snow was tumbling down the mountainside, gathering a frightening amount of force with each second.

George gasped, ashen-faced. "An avalanche! And it's right on the trail Luke's taken!"

Chapter

Sixteen

SNOW ROLLED DOWN the mountain as the lodge shook from the rumbling of the avalanche. The whole world appeared to be tumbling down the slope.

George grabbed frantically for her jacket and cross-country skis, and Nancy, Ned, Liz, and Gunther did likewise. "If Luke's trapped, we have to get to him as fast as we can," Liz said. "You can breathe for only so long under six feet of snow."

She looked at Bess. "You don't ski well enough, so just take care of things back here." Her face was serious. "We'd better be careful. There's no way of knowing how much more snow will fall. We could get trapped ourselves."

"That's one risk we'll just have to take!" George said fiercely.

Then Michael spoke up quietly. "Maybe we shouldn't rush out there like this." He looked around at the others' stunned faces. "Are you sure you want to risk your lives to save a murderer who's already done his best to kill again?"

"I'm sure!" George cried. "And he's not a killer!"

"Whether he is or not, we can't abandon him under an avalanche. Now, let's get going!" Nancy said, and grabbed her ski poles and started after Liz.

"Be careful!" Bess called.

Nancy, Ned, Liz, Michael, and Gunther fought their way forward, the snow stinging their faces. "Are you sure Luke would have gone this way?" Nancy shouted to Liz.

"Absolutely! It's the fastest trail."

They searched for some sign of Luke, but the snow had already covered any tracks. Tears were freezing on George's face. Ned forged doggedly along beside Nancy. If his ankle hurt, he was not letting it hold him back.

Just when it seemed as if they were going to fight through the storm forever, Liz skied around a curve, and Nancy heard her cry out.

They shot ahead to find her staring at an immense pile of snow—the avalanche. "Spread out!" Liz ordered, "and keep your eyes peeled!"

Silently, they obeyed, although the sky was almost as dark as it was at twilight. Michael, ignoring Liz's instructions, skied ahead and then doubled back.

"I've been all the way to the other side of the

avalanche, and I didn't see a thing. We might as well give up. I think I heard more rumbling."

But at that moment, George let out a yelp. She tore past Michael and fell to the ground, clawing frantically at the snow. As Nancy rushed to join her, she saw the tip of a ski protruding from the snow. "That must be him!" she cried, dropping down at George's side.

Feverishly, they all dug around the ski until Luke's leg appeared, then his torso, and then his whole body. He was icy cold, and a dark trickle of frozen blood came from his nose. George ripped Luke's ski jacket open and pressed her ear against his chest. "He's breathing. Barely," she said hoarsely. "We have to get him back to the lodge, and fast!"

The trip back was ominously slow as they took turns supporting Luke's limp weight on a make-shift stretcher made of coats and ski poles. With what felt like a hundred stops and starts, they reached Webb Cove Lodge.

Bess had the fire roaring. They carried Luke in and laid him on a couch in front of it. George stayed by his side, chafing his hands. "All we can do is keep him warm," she finally said, a tremor in her voice. She swallowed hard and hid her face in her hands.

The others had seen Luke's twisted leg and the blood on his face, and knew what she wasn't saying. He could have broken bones, or worse.

"We can't just sit here and wait!" Nancy said fiercely. She jumped up. "I'm going for help."

"Not alone!" Ned said immediately.

"Two people should go," Michael suggested. "George should stay here with Luke. So how about you and me, Nancy?"

"Wait," Ned and Gunther both said at once. "I should go, too," Ned insisted.

"Not with your ankle," Nancy told him.

"What about me?" Gunther said.

Nancy thought for a moment. On the one hand, it might be better to get Gunther as far away from Luke as possible. On the other hand, Gunther didn't know the area as well as Michael. If he got them lost, Luke was as good as dead.

"I think you should stay here, too," Nancy said. "If Michael and I aren't back in an hour, you and Liz can set out as a backup rescue team."

"We should head for the Overlook," Michael said. "The power's on there, and they can call for help. If we cut through the tall trees, we'll get some protection in case there's another avalanche."

Nancy and Michael stepped outside and snapped on their cross-country skis. They set off through the howling wind, Michael in the lead. He skied rapidly, so Nancy had to work hard to keep up with him. After fifteen minutes, Michael halted and turned to look at her. "How are you doing?" he called, smiling.

Nancy drew to a stop beside him. "All right."

"Just all right?" There was a teasing, admiring note in his voice. Michael's mood, considering the circumstances, seemed a bit too happy.

"What are you smiling about?" Nancy asked.

Michael laughed. "Oh, come on! The two of us alone together, speeding through the storm on a dangerous mission. What more could anyone want?"

"Maybe to have a friend survive," Nancy answered grimly.

Michael frowned. "Luke Ericsen, or whatever he says his name is, brought his fate on himself."

"If you mean Berntsen, say so."

"Funny your catching on to that." Michael pushed off expertly and skied quickly down a small slope.

Nancy caught up with him and stopped him. "I didn't have to catch on. He admitted everything to George."

"So his memory's coming back, is it?"

"How did you know he lost his memory?" Nancy asked, a chill running up her spine.

Instead of answering, Michael skied away, intent on reaching the top of the next rise. At its crest he balanced lightly and turned to wait for Nancy. "Look," he said as she joined him, sounding annoyed. "Just because we're being angels of mercy for the guy, do we have to talk about him? It's ruining the whole trip!"

Nancy stared at Michael in disbelief. "You're really enjoying this, aren't you?" she asked incredulously.

"I always enjoy danger!" A glint of excitement danced in his eyes again. "Admit it, that's what real living is all about. Taking risks. Only the weak accept defeat!"

Nancy shuddered. What was going on with Michael? He was acting very strange, and she was scared to find out why. She dug her poles into the snow and, pushing off in a burst of speed, flew past Michael down the slope.

Immediately, Michael was after her. "Nancy!" he called. "You're not being logical. Luke tried to kill George! If he dies from the avalanche, it would spare everyone—including the two of them—the pain of a trial."

Nancy stopped suddenly. "How did you know what happened to George last night?" she asked.

"Liz told me." Michael sounded so cool, so honest.

But Nancy was afraid.

"I'll lead the way," Michael said. "We're getting to a dangerous part of the trail."

As they skied on, Nancy realized that they were headed in the same direction that she and Ned had taken the night before in search of George. Finally, she recognized the spot on Lookout Ledge where George and her masked attacker had struggled.

"Isn't there an easier way to go?" Nancy shouted.

"This is fastest," Michael shouted back. "It's risky, but we're both good skiers. We'll make it."

Nancy paused, eyeing the ledge uneasily.

Michael laughed. "You go first," he suggested. "Then I'll be able to help if you have trouble."

Cautiously, Nancy eased herself onto the narrow ledge. As she rounded a curve, a chunk of the ledge broke off beneath the tip of her ski and tumbled downward. She gasped and leaned back, her heart pounding. There was no choice but to go on, though. She pushed off again.

Nancy felt as if she'd skied Mount Everest when she finally got to the bottom of the slope. Turning to watch Michael flying gracefully down the path along the cliff face, Nancy was amazed at how easy he made it look. He passed her, stopped, and pushed off again. First his right leg, then his left, expertly zipping around a tree.

Suddenly Nancy froze. She'd seen that same fabulous technique before—when the masked stranger had escaped after the murderous attack on George!

As if he felt her eyes boring into him, Michael's perfect style wavered. Not much, but just enough to make him misjudge an overhanging branch in the gloomy light of the storm. He crashed into it and went sprawling.

As he climbed to his feet, muttering exasperatedly, a small black object fell out of his pocket. Not noticing, he brushed himself off and skied on.

Nancy skied over and picked it up. It was a little black box, a remote control device of the sort used in TV shows about spies and cops . . . *and bombs.*

Suddenly Nancy's breath caught in her throat. I've been so stupid, she chided herself. Michael's been right in front of my nose, and I've completely missed seeing the truth. *He's* the killer. He's insane. And now I'm stuck alone with him, in a forest, in the middle of a blizzard.

Chapter

Seventeen

THE EDGES OF the little black box cut into Nancy's hand as she clutched it. A bomb control. Michael probably hadn't set a big bomb, just one large enough to cause a few tremors on the snow-covered mountain. Enough to send down an avalanche to bury Luke Ericsen (and Jon Berntsen) without a trace. Nancy thrust the box into her pocket and set off after Michael.

Michael was the prowler, the one setting the death traps around Webb Cove, the masked attacker who'd almost killed George.

The case ran through Nancy's mind. Everything was becoming crystal clear. Michael had been lying all along, and poor Luke had had to take the rap for him.

Nancy wasn't sure why Michael was determined to kill Luke, but she knew it must have to do with Dieter Mueller's death. Was he bent on revenge for his dead friend, as she had suspected earlier?

Nancy had the feeling it was much more sinister than that. Clearly, Michael had set the first few traps—the broken rope tow, the loose bindings, the Jeep crash—for Luke. He'd probably written the word MURDERER in the snow to scare Luke and to shake him up.

But then he'd turned on George, deliberately disguising himself as Luke and trying to strangle her. There could be just one reason—because she knew who Luke really was, and she realized that *Michael* was to blame for the "accidents." And if Michael realized that Nancy had figured that out, too, he'd turn on her next.

However, he'd then have to get rid of a whole lot of people—everyone who knew that Luke was Jon Berntsen—everyone at Webb Cove.

All at once, Nancy was terrified for her friends back at the lodge. Had Michael planned for something to happen to them after he'd left Webb Cove? She shivered.

Nancy's thoughts raced through her mind as she herself raced along on Michael's trail. She must not, *must not,* let him guess what she knew! Nancy kept on skiing expertly while one thought filled her mind. How was she going to get away from Michael Price? Her friends' lives—and her own—depended on it.

Nancy peered ahead. Oddly, nothing looked familiar. At last, mercifully, the trail widened for several yards. With a burst of speed, Nancy shot past Michael. She had to reach the hotel ahead of him! Desperately, using all her will, concentration, and skill, she skied as she'd never skied before.

But as good as Nancy was, Michael was better. He swooped after her. Nancy streaked through the storm, only too aware that Michael was right on her tail . . . and gaining.

The trail narrowed, corkscrewing into a curve. Nancy poled around it—and a hideous realization struck her. Among all the little hills between Webb Cove and the Overlook Hotel, she had lost her way. But Michael hadn't. Using a circular route, he'd lured her back to Lookout Ledge, where an accident would be *so* plausible.

With a chill, Nancy imagined it all. Michael would reach the Overlook, distraught, claiming that Nancy had had a fatal accident.

There was no way for her to escape. She was at the edge of a precipice, with Michael blocking her path. He stood there smiling, slowly removing his ski goggles as if he had all the time in the world. "You passed the turnoff about a quarter of a mile back. Not surprising in this weather, but too bad."

For a moment their eyes met, and everything was very still.

"Why did you do it?" Nancy asked quietly.

Michael's eyes changed, as if he couldn't believe her stupidity. "For a gold medal, of course!" he sneered. "I deserved to be on the U.S. ski team more than Berntsen did! But at least I was a runner-up. If he got hurt, or died

140

. . . Then I heard him in the Broken Leg Café, challenging Dieter Mueller to that stupid night race. There was my chance!"

Nancy never took her eyes off Michael's. "You mean *you* were trying to kill *Jon?* Then why did you rig Dieter's skis?"

Michael shrugged. "They were a similar model. It was dark and I made a mistake. I watched the whole 'accident' from behind a tree on the slope. I didn't realize I'd rigged the wrong skis until I saw Dieter go down instead of Jon.

"But it turned out not to matter after all, because then I had the chance to kill *two* birds with one stone. I could take care of Berntsen, and eliminate some major Olympic competition at the same time. Too bad about Dieter. I didn't really mean to kill him—just disable him."

He shrugged again, as though the fatality didn't matter.

"How did you pull it off?" Nancy asked, trying to keep Michael talking.

"It was great!" Michael laughed. "Berntsen passed Mueller lying in the snow, so he put on the brakes and climbed back up to see if the guy was all right. I could tell from the look on Berntsen's face that he wasn't. Then Berntsen looked at Mueller's ski—"

Michael took a deep breath, almost in pride. "I knew I'd have to do something fast! I didn't know if Berntsen had seen me hiding in the woods, but I was sure he'd go for help. When he did, I was ready.

"He skied past where I was hiding, and I stuck

out one of my poles and tripped him. While his face was in the snow, I hit his head with a stone."

Michael shook his head.

"I thought they were both dead—so it came as a nasty surprise to learn that Berntsen had survived. But he had amnesia. Then somebody started the rumor that Berntsen had rigged the race and the accident to eliminate Mueller as competition."

I'll bet you started it! Nancy thought, silently accusing Michael.

"It was perfect—except that the scandal wrecked the morale of our team. I didn't even get a bronze," Michael said ruefully. "I told myself, so what? All I had to do was wait four more years for the next Olympics.

"Berntsen dropped out of sight. He had amnesia, anyway, so I didn't have to worry that he'd open his mouth about what had happened. Then I came here to do some skiing, and got the shock of my life when I spotted Berntsen on the slopes one day.

"I asked around, and learned that he was the new ski instructor at Webb Cove Lodge, except that he was using some other name. A little spying told me something else. Old Jon was beginning to get his memory back. I knew I had to get rid of him before he remembered what really happened in Colorado."

Nancy stood silently at the edge of the cliff. The more involved Michael became in his story, the less attention he was paying to Nancy. She hoped that would give her the opportunity she so desperately needed to escape.

Michael smiled crookedly. "So I rigged the rope tow," he continued, "and *you* got on it! I tried to be a hero, but rescuing you brought me face-to-face with Berntsen. And he mentioned the Broken Leg Café.

"That meant it was only a matter of time before he recovered from his amnesia. The worst thing, though, was that he started seeing George. She helped him remember more and more every day. I *had* to shut him up—and her, too, once she learned enough."

Michael sighed, the sound almost lost in the whistling wind. "I really did like you, Nancy. I'm sorry, but . . ."

Michael paused, gathering his strength. The next few seconds seemed to last an eternity. Then, as Nancy had known he would, Michael lunged toward her.

Chapter

Eighteen

As MICHAEL MOVED, so did Nancy. She fell sideways, calling on her gymnastics skill to guide her away from the cliff edge. As she went down, one hand scooped up a handful of snow. The other went to her ski bindings, snapping one, then the second, free.

Michael was still hampered by his skis. Even so, his coordination was superb. He landed beside Nancy, righting himself swiftly.

But Nancy was a split second ahead of him. She flung the snowball in his face. As it hit, momentarily blinding him, she darted behind him and swung her ski pole across his throat, locking it against him in a choke-hold.

Michael began to struggle. One of his hands flailed wildly, groping for her arm. But Nancy jerked the pole tighter. Michael made a muffled coughing sound, and then he sagged against her. Nancy held the viselike grip for a full minute, not daring to risk another of his tricks. Finally, she released the pressure. He slid to her feet in a heap.

Nancy leaned back against a tree, shaking with relief. She was still there moments later when she heard voices calling her name hollowly through the wind. "Here," she gasped hoarsely.

Within minutes, she was in Ned's arms. Liz was there, too, bending over Michael. Nancy was relieved that she could stop suspecting Liz. If Liz had behaved strangely, it must have been from tension. After all, prowlers and accidents and would-be murderers were not everyday happenings, and some people held up under strain better than other people did. She could stop suspecting Gunther, too. The only "evidence" against him had been circumstantial.

"Is he dead?" Nancy asked through cracked lips.

Liz shook her head. "He's alive but out cold. That must have been some stunt you pulled!"

"He was the one who tried to kill Luke . . . and then George, and me, too."

"Shh. We know," Ned whispered. He held her tightly, his lips pressed against her hair.

It was not until they were at the Overlook Hotel, waiting for the police to question Nancy and for rescue squads to attend to both Luke and Michael, that she was able to find out why Ned and Liz had come out in the forest looking for her.

Nancy and Ned were sitting in front of the hotel fireplace, their hands clasped gently, when she asked him about it.

"Luke regained consciousness," Ned said. "He hit his head during the avalanche, and somehow the blow jarred away his amnesia!

"He remembered all about Dieter Mueller's accident, how after Dieter fell he was hurt but still alive, how he'd discovered the missing screw in Dieter's bindings . . . and how he'd noticed Michael Price hiding in the trees farther down the slope. Of course, he didn't suspect that Michael would try to hurt him as he skied down to get help for Dieter. And he never remembered any of it—until today."

Nancy shuddered. "It's hard to believe anyone would do such horrible things."

"But Michael did," Ned exclaimed. "And when Liz and I realized that you were out there alone with a murderer, we took off after you, skiing like maniacs."

"It was wonderful seeing you two come through those trees," Nancy said with a sigh.

"You managed to take pretty good care of Michael without our help, though," Ned said, smiling.

Soon after that, the police arrived to take Nancy's, Ned's, and Liz's statements. Afterward, an officer drove them to the county hospital, where George, Bess, and Gunther were keeping a vigil over Luke. Bess looked haggard, and Nancy knew that she felt both relieved at Gunther's innocence in the case, and guilty at having suspected him.

Michael had regained consciousness, but he wasn't talking. "And not just because of that bad sore throat you gave him," the police lieutenant said to Nancy. "We've been on the phone with the Colorado police and the German embassy. Price is going to need a very high-powered lawyer!"

Luke was in surgery, having suffered not only a broken leg and a couple of crushed ribs, but internal injuries.

It wasn't until dawn that a nurse came into the visitors' lounge, smiling. "Mr. Berntsen's regained consciousness." She looked at Ned. "He's asking for someone named George."

George leaped up and rushed down the corridor with a cry of joy. The nurse, who'd obviously expected a boy to respond to Luke's call, was mildly astonished.

A few hours later, when the others were finally allowed into the room, George was still there, holding Luke's hand tightly. Luke looked haggard, but for the first time since they'd met him, he seemed at peace. His eyes lit up as Nancy came in.

"I guess I owe you a big apology for the way I've treated you," he said. "The first day, when I overheard that you were a detective, I—I just freaked out. The way you poked into things, I was sure that if you started investigating me, I'd end up in jail, even though I hadn't killed Dieter.

"But George tells me Price is going behind bars now, so I want to thank you, sincerely and deeply." Luke smiled almost shyly.

"You know, Luke," Nancy told him, "you're all right!" Then she giggled. "I guess we'll have to get used to calling you Jon Berntsen, won't we? At least, if we're going to see any more of you."

"Oh, you'll see me," Luke assured her. He and George exchanged loving glances. Then George turned scarlet, and the others laughed.

"One more question, if you don't mind," Nancy said.

"Go ahead," Luke replied.

"Didn't you ever wonder if you might have been guilty? After all, you had amnesia and you couldn't remember what you'd done just before and during the race."

"No way," Luke said. "Dieter and I were friends, good friends, even if we were always competing with each other."

"You never suspected that anyone might get hurt in the night race?"

Luke sighed. "I should have. The other people at the Broken Leg thought I was crazy! The worst part was knowing that everyone else believed I'd killed Dieter—and not remembering enough to prove them wrong."

"I never thought you killed him," George cut in.

Luke smiled. "Yeah, but I think you and my mother are the only two people who can truly say that." He laughed. "Anyway, I was determined to remember. And it was starting to happen!

Every once in a while I'd get a flash of memory. Nothing clear, just a feeling that when Mueller and I had had our accidents, somebody else had been there."

He turned to Nancy. "Then you had your 'accident' on the rope tow, and all of a sudden there were three people there, too—me, you, and Michael. It was like I was reliving a memory: seeing an unconscious body and then Michael. I had this flash, a picture of his face, smiling—sneering—at Dieter and me as we argued in the Broken Leg Café."

"So you asked him about it," Nancy prompted.

"And he denied it," Luke said. "But I kept getting more disturbing flashes. I felt sure that Price had more to do with what had happened to Mueller and me than he was saying. But I had no proof." His face softened. "And then George recognized me. And she believed in me."

"Why didn't you tell me?" Nancy exclaimed. "I could have helped! And we might have been able to wrap this case up before so many people got hurt!"

George just looked at Nancy. "You didn't like Luke, remember? Would you have trusted the word of someone accused of being a murderer? The only reason he wasn't prosecuted in Colorado was because the police didn't have proof, not because they didn't have suspicions!"

"And then he disappeared," Ned added. "That must have looked plenty suspicious!"

"All the same," Nancy said softly, "I wish you'd told me. I *trust* you."

"Do you?" George asked evenly. "You didn't tell me what you were finding out about Luke or the murderer. I was going nuts, not knowing."

"It sounds to me," Gunther said, "as if you two had a language gap, the way I did when I first came to this country. I had studied English, but I had—what do you call it?—a communications problem."

"That's it exactly," Nancy said ruefully. She smiled at George, and George smiled back.

"Hey," Ned said, rising and pulling Nancy up with him, "now that the storm's over and we can go out in the snow again, you people don't mind if we desert you, do you? We have things to do and places to go." He threw Nancy a teasing smile.

"Where?" Nancy asked, grinning.

"You'll see," Ned answered vaguely.

They went out into the early morning sun. The storm had ended and the trees, covered with glittering ice, shone silver in the light. Ned waited until they had reached the car to take Nancy in his arms and kiss her. "Come on!" he said exuberantly.

"Where?"

"Back to the hotel Jacuzzi! The rest of the gang won't think of it, so it's the one place we can count on being alone. We have," he added, kissing her again, "a lot of vacationing to catch up on!"

Nancy's Next Case:

Working undercover for a hot new teen magazine, Nancy's assignment is to protect the publisher . . . from murder.

She's also trying to save her relationship with Ned. He's tired of taking a backseat to every case that comes along, and he's met a girl more interested in him than in mysteries.

Nancy must risk losing her love—and her life—in *SMILE AND SAY MURDER*, Case #4 in *The Nancy Drew Files.*™

HAVE YOU SEEN
NANCY DREW®
LATELY?

THE NANCY DREW FILES™

1 SECRETS CAN KILL 64193/$2.75
2 DEADLY INTENT 64393/$2.75
3 MURDER ON ICE 64194/$2.75
4 SMILE AND SAY MURDER 64585/$2.75
5 HIT AND RUN HOLIDAY 64394/$2.75
6 WHITE WATER TERROR 64586/$2.75
7 DEADLY DOUBLES 62543/$2.75
8 TWO POINTS FOR MURDER 63079/$2.75
9 FALSE MOVES 63076/$2.75
#10 BURIED SECRETS 63077/$2.75
#11 HEART OF DANGER 63078/$2.75
#12 FATAL RANSOM 62644/$2.75
#13 WINGS OF FEAR 64137/ $2.75
#14 THIS SIDE OF EVIL 64139/$2.75
#15 TRIAL BY FIRE 64139/$2.75
#16 NEVER SAY DIE 64140/$2.75
#17 STAY TUNED FOR DANGER 64141/$2.75
#18 CIRCLE OF EVIL 64142/$2.75
#19 SISTERS IN CRIME 64225/$2.75
#20 VERY DEADLY YOURS 64226/$2.75
#21 RECIPE FOR MURDER 64227/$2.75
#22 FATAL ATTRACTION 64228/$2.75
#23 SINISTER PARADISE 64229/$2.75
#24 TILL DEATH DO US PART 64230/$2.75

Simon & Schuster, Mail Order Dept. ASB
200 Old Tappan Rd., Old Tappan, N.J. 07675

Please send me the books I have checked above. I am enclosing $_____ (please add 75¢ to cover postage and handling for each order. N.Y.S. and N.Y.C. residents please add appropriate sales tax). Send check or money order—no cash or C.O.D.'s please. Allow up to six weeks for delivery. For purchases over $10.00 you may use VISA: card number, expiration date and customer signature must be included.

Name _____

Address _____

City _____ State/Zip _____

VISA Card No. _____ Exp. Date _____

Signature _____ 119-04

NANCY DREW® AND THE HARDY BOYS®
TEAM UP FOR MORE MYSTERY...
MORE THRILLS...AND MORE
EXCITEMENT THAN EVER BEFORE!

A NANCY DREW & HARDY BOYS
S u p e r M y s t e r y
by Carolyn Keene

In the NANCY DREW AND HARDY BOYS SuperMystery, Nancy's unique sleuthing and Frank and Joe's hi-tech action-packed approach make for a dynamic combination you won't want to miss!

Join Nancy and the Hardys as they team up for a big new adventure in:

☐ **DOUBLE CROSSING**
64917/$2.95

Simon & Schuster Mail Order Dept. NHS
200 Old Tappan Rd., Old Tappan, N.J. 07675

Please send me the books I have checked above. I am enclosing $_____ (please add 75¢ to cover postage and handling for each order. N.Y.S. and N.Y.C. residents please add appropriate sales tax). Send check or money order—no cash or C.O.D.'s please. Allow up to six weeks for delivery. For purchases over $10.00 you may use VISA: card number, expiration date and customer signature must be included.

Name_____

Address_____

City _____ State/Zip _____

VISA Card No._____ Exp. Date_____

Signature _____150-02

HAVE YOU SEEN THE HARDY BOYS® LATELY?

THE HARDY BOYS ©
CASE FILES

#1 DEAD ON TARGET 67258/$2.75
#2 EVIL, INC. 67259/$2.75
#3 CULT OF CRIME 67260/$2.75
#4 THE LAZARUS PLOT 62129/$2.75
#5 EDGE OF DESTRUCTION 62646/$2.75
#6 THE CROWNING TERROR 62647/$2.75
#7 DEATHGAME 62648/$2.75
#8 SEE NO EVIL 62649/$2.75
#9 THE GENIUS THIEVES 63080/$2.75
#10 HOSTAGES OF HATE 63081/$2.75
#11 BROTHER AGAINST BROTHER
     63082/$2.75
#12 PERFECT GETAWAY 63083/$13.75
#13 THE BORGIA DAGGER 64463/$2.75
#14 TOO MANY TRAITORS
     64460/$2.75
#15 BLOOD RELATIONS
     64461/$2.75
#16 LINE OF FIRE
     64462/$2.75

Simon & Schuster, Mail Order Dept. ASD
200 Old Tappan Rd., Old Tappan, N.J. 07675

Please send me the books I have checked above. I am enclosing $_____ (please add 75¢ to cover
postage and handling for each order. N.Y.S. and N.Y.C. residents please add appropriate sales tax). Send
check or money order—no cash or C.O.D.'s please. Allow up to six weeks for delivery. For purchases over
$10.00 you may use VISA: card number, expiration date and customer signature must be included.

Name _____

Address _____

City _____ State/Zip _____

VISA Card No. _____ Exp. Date _____

Signature _____120-05